The Gunslinger

RED RIDGE CHRONICLES BOOK 1

SARAH LAMB

Contents

		V
1.	Chapter 1	1
2.	Chapter 2	9
3.	Chapter 3	15
4.	Chapter 4	23
5.	Chapter 5	29
6.	Chapter 6	35
7.	Chapter 7	43
8.	Chapter 8	49
9.	Chapter 9	57
10.	Chapter 10	65
11.	Chapter 11	73

12. Chapter 12   79

13. Chapter 13   87

14. Chapter 14   91

15. Chapter 15   97

16. Chapter 16   103

17. Chapter 17   107

18. Chapter 18   111

19. Chapter 19   117

20. Chapter 20   125

21. Epilogue   129

22. What's next?   133

23. Note from Author   135

24. Want a Free Red Ridge Chronicles Prequel?   137

25. Read or Listen to the Red Ridge Chronicles   139
    Books

26. About the Author   141

To each of the special people who have helped me bring this series and many of my other books to life: Brooke, for her on-point suggestions and proofreading; Nancy, for her fantastic covers; Spencer, for his incredible narration; and you, dear readers, for your endless support.

Chapter 1

1870s Oregon

"Shoot first, ask questions later."

"Now, Gus," Hannah Carson sighed. "Don't say that. Especially around Meg." She glanced over at her four-year-old daughter, who was wrapping her rag doll in a blanket. While her daughter hadn't seemed to notice the old ranch hand's comment, she didn't want her repeating such things.

"I'm telling you, that's what you do with men like that," old Gus retorted. "I'm not leaving you while he's here." He folded his tanned, thin arms, heavily corded with veins, and leaned against the wall. "If I were a young man again," he muttered, and then mumbled something so low Hannah couldn't hear him.

Laying a hand on his arm and giving a gentle squeeze, Hannah nodded. She appreciated the gesture more than he likely knew, and tried to steel herself as Wallace Carson, her former brother-in-law, rode closer onto the property, approaching the house on his black mare.

"I'm going outside to talk with him," she said, her voice quiet. If it quivered a little, Gus pretended not to notice.

"Not alone, you ain't," he said.

"Please, Gus. Look after Meg. Keep her inside."

Gus frowned, the wrinkles in his weathered face growing deeper as he looked between Hannah and her daughter. Through the kitchen window, they could see Wallace dismount. "Fine," he said. "But I'm staying near the window to hear. You scream, I'll come a running. Won't let him keep bothering you."

With a short nod, Hannah stepped through the kitchen door and into the yard. She left her apron on, not wanting Wallace to think he was welcome or worth looking nice for. She left the door cracked so Gus could hear better. "Wallace," she greeted, her voice neutral.

"Hannah. Came to see if you'd made up your mind," he greeted, stepping close.

For a man with such an important question to ask, he sure didn't seem like he cared at all about his appearance, she thought. He looked like he'd been out working in the fields all day, even though he never lifted a finger unless it was to boss someone else around.

Under his cowboy hat she knew sat a curly head full of graying brown hair filled with grease. His shirt was stained, with wet splotches under the arms and across his chest. The hem of his pants and the bottoms of his boots were mucky. She knew it wasn't mud. They'd not had rain for well over a week now, though she wished it would pour, just so he'd leave.

That wasn't to be, though. The sun shone brightly, the sky was a perfect-colored blue, and it was all in stark contrast to the gloom the man brought with him. Hannah steeled herself and shook her head. "I'm not marrying you, Wallace. I've told you that."

As if he didn't hear her, Wallace walked a few paces to the left and stared out at the field where a few dozen cattle grazed. He let his gaze roam over them, then turned, taking in the large garden and the barn, where inside four horses resided. A chicken wandered in the yard, pecking her way past, a chick following close behind. It was a feisty hen, and for a moment, Hannah let herself wish it would peck at her unwanted visitor.

Wallace looked back at her. "You can't run this place on your own," he told her. "It's too much for you."

"I'm not on my own. I have Gus," Hannah said calmly.

"That's not what I meant." Wallace gave her a hard look. "You don't have a husband. You don't have a son. The land defaults back to my family, now that Jim's gone."

Hannah knew that. She'd always known that. Jim had told her before they were married, his fifty acres and all he had belonged to the family. The only way to keep it was for him to have a son. Then, it would rightfully pass to him. If something were to happen to him, it went back to his brother and his brother's sons. Right now, Wallace had two, both in their twenties. Jim had been the youngest of six, so he was twelve years younger than his brother, and the only other boy.

At the time, she hadn't worried about it at all. Jim was strong, healthy. So it was unexpected when, one day, he was attacked by a bear in the barn. Jim had shot it, but not before he'd been clawed badly. The wounds had gotten infected, and the doctor couldn't help him. He'd died a few short weeks later, and his brother had been by several times since.

Each visit made during the last six months since Jim's death had been the same. Asking her to marry him, and then threatening her when she said no. She half wondered if he was as tired of this as she was. Still, he didn't give up in his persistence, and neither would she give in.

"You've no other option," Wallace said. "Where would you go? You can't stay here. This isn't your land anymore." He smirked. "There's a nice spot waiting for you in my bed. Just say yes."

With a shudder running down her spine, Hannah threw back her shoulders. From the day she'd first met Wallace, she couldn't stand him. It might have been the way he leered at her, and every other woman he saw. It might have been the fact he'd always been jealous of his hard-working brother, who was their father's favorite. It could even be that she just didn't like him. She never could tell, but there was no way Hannah was marrying him. He'd worked his first wife into her grave. Everyone knew it. The woman had near wasted away. He treated her as little more than a slave. Hannah had met her once, just before she married Jim. The woman hadn't spoken once. She was bone-thin, paler than a cup of milk, and had hollow eyes. Hannah didn't want that to be her.

"I'm out of patience," Wallace snarled. "Marry me, today. Or leave."

"I can't," Hannah said, her voice firm. She was pleased it wasn't shaking. Her shoulders back, she fixed him with a cool stare. "I've every right to be here. I've spoken with the lawyer."

"No, you don't," he argued. His voice grew loud, and behind her, Hannah could hear Gus at the window moving closer. Without even turning around, she knew the old man was glaring at the man who he loathed as much as she did. She just hoped, for his sake and hers, he wouldn't do anything foolish.

"I do," she answered calmly. "You see, I don't know yet that I don't have a son." She placed her hand gently on her stomach, her eyes fixed onto Wallace's. "I have until my child is born before I either need to leave, or he claims the land."

Wallace's mouth opened and closed for a moment before he snarled, "That's what you think." He climbed back on his horse and turned it sharply.

As he rode out, the cloud of dust rising behind him, Hannah watched. She couldn't feel triumphant. She didn't dare. While she hoped for a son to give him his father's inheritance, she knew that wasn't something she had control of.

A shadow fell, and she looked over at Gus next to her.

"His face when you told him that," he chuckled.

Hannah didn't answer. She hadn't cared about Wallace's shocked expression. No, what concerned her was the hard look in his eyes, and the anger laced in his words. "That's what you think," he'd said.

Was that a threat? To her or to her unborn child? What kind of a man would do that?

But Hannah didn't even have to ask herself that. She knew. Wallace would. The man was as evil as they came, and he'd always been envious that this land, Jim's land, was better than his own. But he was right about one thing. She really didn't have any options. If her child wasn't male, there was nothing else she could do, because Hannah refused to marry Wallace Carson.

But would she be safe until then? Hannah glanced at Gus. She was sure worry was written on her face. It was hard not to be concerned. His single headshake, also showing his concern, didn't make her feel one bit better.

"He'll be back," Gus sighed, and turned back toward the barn. He muttered as he walked, "Men like him don't never give up."

Hannah wrapped her arms tightly around herself. "And I don't know how to stop him," she whispered.

Chapter 2

Sitting at the kitchen table, Hannah put her head into her hands and sighed. What was she going to do? As much as she hated to admit it, Wallace was right about another thing too. It wasn't just that she didn't have options. The property really was too much for her and Gus to manage on their own.

Oh, it's not that she hadn't tried to get help. She and Gus had gone all over, asking for hands. They even had a small bunkhouse that could be used, and enough money to employ two or three men until profits could be made. But Wallace Carson had made enough threats and promises to anyone who even so much as sniffed around her request that no one would come. No matter what she offered to pay. Son or no son, it was only a matter of time before it was all too much. She couldn't sell; the land had to be passed from father to son.

A feeling of desperation rose, and Hannah closed her eyes. For a long moment, she allowed a wave of self-indulgent pity to wash over her. Meg was asleep, so she'd never know her mama wasn't as strong as she pretended to be. A tear slipped down her cheek. She wished Jim were here. He'd know what to do.

But of course, if Jim were here, she wouldn't have this problem.

Hannah sat up, wiped her eyes with the back of her hand, and checked on the loaf of bread in the oven. The yeasty aroma filled the air and made her stomach growl. There was plenty of freshly churned butter to go with a warm slice, but she was making herself wait until tomorrow for it. Perhaps she'd even add some drizzles of honey as a treat for herself. Goodness knew she deserved one, after the day she'd had.

The open window let in a welcome breeze, and the soft sound of crickets singing set a steady beat. Hannah listened for a long moment, losing herself in their song. It soothed her, and she let out a yawn.

She'd go to bed once the bread was done, though she wasn't in a hurry. Who knew what tomorrow would bring? She sure didn't, and wasn't the least bit anxious for it to arrive, but bedtime meant a chance to be alone with her sorrow.

Her mind never seemed to still, always searching for a solution to her problem.

There was a scuffling sound, and Hannah looked up. Gus walked in the kitchen holding a newspaper. He'd been sleeping in the front room these last few weeks, having left the bunkhouse to protect her and Meg when Jim had gone. That was another thing she wasn't sure if he realized meant so much to her. At the same time, though, Hannah worried a little. Gus was nearing seventy. He should be overseeing a group of young men around the ranch, not trying to do it all on his own.

"Something to drink?" Hannah asked, looking up at him. She paused, tilting her head slightly, her hand frozen over the oven. Gus had a strange expression on his face. Excitement, almost. But why?

"Yep. Get some paper and a pencil too," he told her, lowering himself stiffly into one of the kitchen chairs.

Hannah did as he asked, sliding the fresh cider jug onto the table along with two cups, a scrap of paper, and the requested pencil. "You're up to something," she told him. Her eyes narrowed suspiciously. "What?"

"Look here," Gus said proudly, showing her the newspaper. "This here is a paper from one of the big cities. You see what people do?" A finger tapped a row of columns.

Puzzled, Hannah stared at the newspaper a moment. She couldn't spot what it was that had him so excited. Finally, she shook her head. "Read?" she answered.

"No, this," he said impatiently, and tapped again.

Hannah frowned as she looked at the newspaper. She could read, but sometimes she couldn't follow along with Gus's thoughts. It had always amazed her how sharp his mind was, at his advanced age. When they'd first met, she was also surprised at how much of a reader Gus was. He was incredibly proud of the fact, too, since so many others who grew up as ranch hands didn't even know their letters. He bought himself a paper each week, read it front page to back, and then read it all over again. He kept them, too, in a little pile in the bunkhouse.

"Any guesses?" His voice drew her from her thoughts.

She looked closer. "Place ads?" she guessed. At his answering grin, she said, "What does that have to do with us?"

Gus leaned back in his chair proudly. "It's the answer to your problem."

Closing her eyes briefly, Hannah drew in a breath before reopening them. She was tired mentally, physically, and emotionally. The last thing she wanted was one of Gus's riddles, but she humored him. "Go on."

"We can't get nobody to help us, right?" he asked. "Wallace done bought them all off." At her nod, he continued, "Also, you need protecting." Noticing her look of objection, he held up a hand. "I'm not as young as I used to be. You've got a baby on the way. One that's going to decide your fate, and Meg's. Not to mention the baby's. You need protecting."

The look Gus gave her dared her to argue. Hannah couldn't. He was right. He was absolutely right. What she was having trouble following along with though, was his idea. "So we take out an ad?" she asked. "For help?"

"That's right," Gus said. "For a gunslinger."

"A gunslinger." Hannah's voice was flat. Maybe Gus had been outside too long. He wasn't making sense at all. Why in the world would he want to bring such a dangerous type of person here?

"Yep. That's why I asked the general store owner to get me one of these papers sent in special like. Now I've got the address to wire to. I'm going to go into town first thing tomorrow morning and order us a gunslinger."

It was Hannah's turn to sit back into her chair. But her action wasn't one of pride over an idea, but of disbelief. He was acting like you went and picked out a gunslinger like...like fabric for a new dress or a packet of sewing needles.

"Why do we need a gunslinger? Why don't we just place an advertisement for another hand? He can help you, and if there's trouble, he can have his gun out," Hannah said.

"No good," Gus said, the wrinkles on his cheeks creasing deeply as he frowned. "Don't do it. You need someone who won't back down if things get heated. No hand is going to be loyal enough for that to someone who has just hired him. Matter of fact, I think that's how you lost one or two of them. Money talks, girl. Better ours do the talking and hire an expert gunman, not another rancher."

Hannah worried her lip between her teeth. He might have a point. She thought about arguing, not that she was sure it would do any good. Gus was as stubborn as they came. But she also couldn't discount the facts he'd laid out before her. In fact, the more she thought about it, turning it over and over in her mind, the better hiring an expert sounded. Someone who Wallace didn't have in his pocket could be quite valuable. Maybe this gunslinger could even be persuaded to help out a little on the ranch. Or knew someone who could.

Lost in thought, she nodded slowly to herself. It might work. If nothing else, it was something to try. Goodness knew they didn't have many options right now. Hannah picked up the pencil. "Very well. How should we word it?"

Chapter 3

Hannah peered out the kitchen window. Gus was riding up, but with his hat shading his face, she couldn't see his expression. She moved to the door as the horse slowed, and he climbed down and tied it at the water trough.

"Got some good news," he told her.

"That would be welcome," she answered. "Come in, and let me get you a drink."

"Be obliged," Gus answered, taking his hat off as he walked in. He reached into his pocket and handed Meg a pink penny candy. She squealed and hugged him, then looked at her mother pleadingly.

"Go on," Hannah laughed, then she turned to Gus. "You spoil her."

"Don't got one of my own. Need to spoil someone," he answered.

She slid some ginger water toward him. Smacking his lips, he took a long drink. "Got any leftover biscuits? Maybe with honey?" he asked. When Hannah handed them to him, he thanked her, and then reached into his pocket again. Hannah looked curiously at the bundle of papers he pulled out.

"Remember I told you I'd check into those replies we got?" he asked.

"Yes. And I was leaving it to you to choose who you thought was best," she answered.

Not only would Gus know more about this than she would, but it made him feel useful, something she could tell some days he didn't feel, when his aching bones were acting up.

"Well, I contacted a fellow I know, and ran some of the names past him." Gus looked up to make sure she was listening. "He wrote me back today, and said this is who we should pick." He thumbed through the stack and handed her a slip of paper with a name circled.

"Eli Jones," Hannah read. She looked up at Gus. "What can you tell me about him?" She bit her lip. "I'm still a little uncomfortable about the idea, to be honest." She set the paper down between them.

"I know," Gus told her. "But he's the best, I hear. Quick on the draw and sharper than a tack, he's the best of the best in every way. A tracker, a hunter, a gunslinger like few others."

"And we can afford him?" Hannah asked, doubt in her voice. "A man like that must cost a lot."

Gus nodded. "Sure can. He's reasonable priced. Who knows? Might even give you a discount, you being so pretty."

Hannah blushed and looked away. "I'm not expecting that," she mumbled, and stood up to get herself a drink, and hopefully cover her embarrassment.

Maybe it was true that she was pretty. Jim had always told her so, but she didn't have a mirror, only the reflection of the creek to see her face in. She hoped it wasn't aging, with the stress of the last few weeks.

Meg, truthful as all children are, would have surely said something if her light brown hair had begun to streak with gray, and the fact she hadn't was relieving. Widowed at twenty-seven. It happened, but Hannah sure hadn't expected it to happen to her. Not when she had so much life ahead of her.

Or so she hoped, anyway. Who knew, what with Wallace and his threats? There were moments she wondered if she'd make it through the year.

"Well, tell him yes," she answered, looking once more at the paper. "The sooner the better. Let Wallace know we aren't going to be intimidated. I have three months still that I can stay here, and I plan to." She crossed her arms defiantly.

Gus nodded and stood. "Let me wire him today, then. Get him here soon. I'll head back now."

"Wait, let's hitch the wagon," Hannah said. "We'll all go. I want to get some extra supplies, since we'll have another to feed."

"Think it's wise to leave the house alone?" Gus asked.

Hannah paused. Was it? She looked around a moment, her eyes scanning the kitchen with its large cast iron stove, two windows with curtains, a dry sink, and the table and chairs. There wasn't much here, but what she had, she loved and needed.

But then she shook her head. "If Wallace does anything to this place, he's only hurting himself." She pressed her lips together, willing the hurt that flared in her heart to go away, and added, "It could be his soon, and he knows it."

There. She'd said it out loud. It was painful to admit, especially to Gus, but he knew it as well as she did. She couldn't pretend anything else.

"Reckon you're right," Gus answered. He rested his hand on her arm a moment. "I'll hitch up." He turned to the door, then looked back. "Don't you worry, now. Things are going to be just fine."

Hannah nodded. A lump in her throat formed. She wanted to believe his words, but at the moment, she just wasn't sure.

She hurried to get Meg ready. Before long, Meg, her doll, and Hannah were helped into the wagon and set off on the half-hour ride to town.

On the drive, she tried to let her worries go. It was a beautiful day. A light breeze was made as the horses pulled them. It was midsummer, and her favorite time of year. They passed corn and wheat, stretching high to meet the golden sun. Small animals scurried back and forth in the tall grass, and Meg laughed, squealing as she sat between the adults, holding the reins of the two horses like she was driving them herself.

It was moments like these that Hannah didn't have enough of. She swallowed, and her heart ached for Jim. It should be him here, his hands overtop Meg's. In fact, if he were here, she wouldn't be in this position. For a moment, she let herself feel angry. It was easier than feeling sad.

In the distance, the small town rose before them, and Gus took the reins from Meg. He stopped in front of the general store and helped Hannah and Meg down, then pushed up his battered hat. "I'll send this note, then come help you carry your purchases," he told Hannah.

She nodded. "Thank you, Gus." As he set off, she pushed open the door to the store. She always enjoyed coming here. There was just about everything you could want here, and the owner made sure to always get something new in each month.

Stacks of fabric bolts, barrels of dry goods, and the spicy scent of medicinal herbs caught her attention as she walked in.

The kind face of Mrs. Stover looked up from behind the counter, where she was counting buttons. "How are you?" the shopkeeper asked with a smile.

Meg had wandered over to look, her hands carefully folded behind her back, at a display of penny candy, seemingly forgetting that Gus had just given her one. Hannah returned the smile and said, "Well enough, I suppose." She reached into her handbag and pulled out her list. Carefully unfolding it, she held it out. "I'd like these items, please."

Mrs. Stover took the list, inspected it for a moment, nodded, and then leaned in close. "Hannah, I've heard whisperings," she said quietly. "Wallace Carson isn't too happy you are still on that land. He told me I shouldn't sell you anything."

Hannah's shoulders tensed. Was Mrs. Stover against her too? She was a distant cousin, three times removed on Jim's side.

"My son Bill," Mrs. Stover continued softly, "has been keeping an ear out for me. Wish there was something I could do for you," she said. "Wallace owns more than half the town. Whoever he doesn't own, he threatens." She bit her lip and straightened up. Her shoulders squared, Mrs. Stover said, her voice stern, "I told my Bill none of that here. My store is neutral. He agreed. So don't you feel afraid to come in whenever you want. I'll sell you what you need."

"I had not even thought that might not be an option," Hannah said, her voice trembling. She glanced at Meg to make sure she wasn't listening, then back at Mrs. Stover. "Would...would the town run me out at his order?"

Mrs. Stover pressed her lips. "I don't know. I told Wallace that it was a bad idea. He wants to marry you to get that land without a fight. How would it look, starving and threatening you and his little niece? Blood related they are." She nodded at Meg. "Like I said, you watch out, but you don't need to around me."

Hannah's shoulders slumped when Mrs. Stover turned away and started filling her order. Things were worse than she thought. Despite Mrs. Stover's promise, if the merchants stopped selling her supplies, she'd be forced to travel nearly a day's journey to get more.

What would happen if they refused as well? She didn't want to marry Wallace, but what else could she do if her child wasn't a son? How would she take care of Meg?

Biting her lip, she looked over at her daughter, whose face was beaming as Mrs. Stover gifted her a peppermint stick in trade for a hug. She waved it at her mama and giggled. Her smile beamed brightly, so full of innocence and joy. It wasn't just the land. This was also a part of what she was fighting to protect.

That gunslinger couldn't get here soon enough.

Chapter 4

With a critical eye, Hannah stood, hands on her hips, as she glanced around the bunkhouse. She didn't go in there often, there wasn't a need, but the last two days she'd cleaned it out, top to bottom. Every inch had been scrubbed, a pile of extra blankets sat on one of the single beds, and she'd checked the wooden trunk at the bottom to make sure she'd gotten the cobwebs out so the gunslinger would have a place to store his belongings.

He and Gus should be arriving any time. Hannah couldn't help it, she was curious. What was a gunslinger like? Loud? Dirty? Would he chew tobacco and spit frequently? She hoped not. What would his manners be? Rough? What about his language?

Hannah bit her lip in worry. It was too late now to put a stop to him coming, but she hoped, for Meg's sake, he'd watch what he did and said. Perhaps she should have that conversation with him, if Gus hadn't.

"I see 'em, Mama," Meg called from the yard.

Hannah quickly ran out and wrapped an arm around Meg. She didn't want her running toward the horses and getting trampled.

Coming closer, Gus led the way on his chestnut. Behind him, riding in on a large black horse, was the gunslinger. He was too far away for her to get a good look at him. She could see he was sitting tall, and a dark-colored hat was low over his eyes. That was about it. A twinge of worry filled her stomach, but Hannah shook her head, took a deep breath, and pushed that feeling away. Gus had looked into the man, so surely he was all right. He loved Meg as much as she did, and wouldn't dare risk any harm to her.

They pulled up, and Hannah raised her head to study the gunslinger. The sun shone behind the riders, making them nothing but shadow. She held one hand out to shade her eyes. "Welcome," she said simply.

The men swung off their horses. Gus, a little stiffly, and the gunslinger effortlessly. He took off his hat, allowing Hannah a better look at him. Her breath caught as he said, "Ma'am."

Hannah couldn't help but stare. The man was nothing like she'd expected. He was tall, lean, but his forearms, where his shirt sleeves had been rolled up, were corded, showing strength. A light beard was on his chin, and he sported a well-groomed mustache. His brown hair was pushed back from his forehead, and his eyes—his startling, piercing, solemn ice-blue eyes—captured her attention. Hannah had never seen such a color before. Tiny amber specks caught the sunlight. They were near mesmerizing, and it was hard not to look at them.

She'd been staring, she realized that, but thankfully, Meg was there and interrupted her thoughts. "Hello. I'm Meg." Meg stared up at him, her nose scrunched as she squinted into the bright sun.

To Hannah's surprise, the gunslinger knelt down, eye level to Meg. "Hello, Meg. I'm Eli Jones. I'm here to help you and your mama and Gus around the place."

Hannah sagged slightly in relief. Gus promised that would be the story he told everyone and had also promised to make sure the gunslinger did the same.

The greeting seemed to be all Meg wanted. She nodded, and skipped back to the house. Eli rose and nodded again at Hannah, his attention now fully on her.

"Gus filled me in on your situation on the ride back," he said. "I'd like to hear about your concerns and anything else you feel might be valuable information."

"Of course," Hannah said. "However I can help, I will. I'm grateful you came, Mr. Jones."

"Eli," he corrected, a hint of a smile twitching at the corners of his lips. "Eli is fine, ma'am."

"Hannah, then," she said, letting herself smile and relax slightly.

His eyes searched her face for a moment, and he nodded. "Hannah."

There was a sudden jolt in her stomach at her name on his lips. Feeling tongue-tied, she stammered, "C-can I show you the bunkhouse?"

"I'll do that," Gus said. "I'm going to give him a tour of the place. He wants to look around, see the boundaries of the land."

"I'll work on the evening meal, then," Hannah said.

Eli put his hat back on, but tipped it to her and wordlessly followed Gus. Her eyes followed him as they walked toward the barn, leading their horses. Now that he was here, Hannah wasn't sure what to think. She'd imagined an older, grizzled man, much like Gus. Not an attractive man, close to her age. It was a good thing Gus was here. Once word got around how her new "hired hand" looked, it wouldn't be seen as proper.

Hannah went back inside and stirred her simmering stew. An apple pie sat on the window, and she carefully measured some flour and lard to make biscuits.

An hour later, she removed them from the oven and peered through the window. She wondered how far Gus had taken Eli, and when they'd be back. She'd just moved away from the window when the sound of voices faintly trickled through the open door.

There was a note of concern in one, and she stepped outside, her brow furrowing. When Gus and Eli came around the side of the house, they looked grim.

"We got ourselves a problem," Gus said. "Eli got here just in time."

Chapter 5

Hannah chilled as she looked at the two men. Gus looked worried, and Eli's hand rested on his belt, inches away from one of the revolvers he carried. "What's happened?" she asked.

Eli's eyes darted to Meg, who was sitting at the kitchen table, making lines on a slate. Hannah held up a finger, went back in, and gave Meg a biscuit with a dollop of honey. She then came back out, shutting the door behind her.

Gus scratched at his head. "Eli's found some signs someone's been poking around. Recent like, too."

"What do you mean, poking around?" Hannah felt tense. If her words came out a little harsh, she didn't mean for them to. She softened her tone and asked, "What did you find?"

"There are footsteps around the bunkhouse and the barn—a few days old for some, a day for others. They don't match Gus's boots, and I just got here. Someone's been stopping by. Frequently. Since you don't have any workers right now, seems to mean someone's either looking for something or keeping an eye on things here."

"Why would they do either?" Hannah asked, frustrated. "There's nothing to look for. And why would someone be watching to see what I'm doing?"

Eli shrugged. "Maybe to see how desperate you were getting. Maybe to make you become desperate." He nodded at Gus, who grimly held up a pair of reins. Hannah looked at them in puzzlement.

"Near cut through," the old man explained, his voice low. "Weren't like that when we took the wagon to town last week."

Hannah reached out with trembling fingers and inspected the leather straps. Even to her inexperienced eye, she could see that the wear on them wasn't normal. They'd been cut. There was no doubt about that.

Her lips pressed together, and she handed the reins back to Gus.

"I'll repair them," he told her. "But don't you be taking any rides in the wagon or on a horse without me or Eli looking everything over before you go."

"Do you think it was Wallace?" Hannah asked.

Gus shrugged. "Maybe. Could have been one of his men. Let's eat. Sooner you get Meg to sleep, the sooner we get to talk."

***

Meg had worn herself out and was sound asleep, tucked into her little bed in Hannah's room. Hannah, Eli, and Gus sat in the kitchen, their voices low.

"I don't know much about men in your profession," Hannah said. "But we've been told you are the best. And we need your help. I need your help. Is that something you can give? Is this too different from what you usually do?" She looked away for a moment, then back. "Is this too much? Now that you know what we are facing?"

Eli's face took on a serious expression. "I won't lie to you. I've protected people before, and I've tracked down and brought others to justice. This is the first time that I've been hired by a woman to protect her and her unborn child." He shook his head. "Evil man that threatens a woman and her babes."

"That's what he is," Gus agreed. He scraped his chair back. "I'm going to take a walk around the outside of the house and barn before we lock the door for the night."

Hannah nodded and watched as Gus left. Eli raised his mug to his lips and asked, "Why don't you say yes to someone else? Not that man, but another."

"What do you mean?" Hannah asked, puzzled. "Yes to what?"

Eli set his mug down. "Yes to getting married." His tone and expression were curious, yet Hannah almost felt a hint of reproach. Was he upset at his assignment, but too proud to say no?

"I shouldn't have to," she said with a frown. "I might be a woman without much of her own, but one thing I do have is my pride. It's my right to say who I will or won't marry."

"I wasn't trying to upset you," Eli said quickly. "I was just curious. I've not met the man yet, but I have known many women who have married for convenience. Many times, it even works out. You don't think that would be the case here? There's got to be someone who would marry a woman as beautiful as you."

"I know it won't be," Hannah said. Her voice was tight, and she forced herself to ignore his compliment. "Call me foolish, I don't care, but I'd hoped..." She stopped. They'd just met. He didn't need to know all the thoughts in her head. He wouldn't care. Men like him only came to do the job, get paid, and look for the next one.

But when she finally looked up, he was watching, waiting. There was a look in his eyes that wasn't judgmental. It wasn't filled with amusement. There was...concern? Whatever it was made her continue talking before she'd even realized it.

"I'd hoped for love. You see, Jim, my husband, *was* a marriage of convenience."

Eli leaned back then, arms crossed, and shook his head. "I find it hard to believe that a woman like you had to have a marriage of convenience."

Before she could ask him what he meant, Gus walked in. "Didn't see nothing," he said. He poured more cider and sat.

"It's late," Eli said. "Gus, we are taking watches. Can you take the first one? Two hours on, two hours off until daylight?"

Gus straightened his shoulders. "Sure can. Nothing's going to get through me if I can help it." He gestured outside. "I'll start walking around. Do some circles around the house. I might be old, but my hearing's right sharp still."

"Thank you," Hannah said softly. "If you need anything, please come and get it."

The door closed behind him as he left, and Eli rose to follow. "We'll talk more tomorrow," he said. At her nod, he moved to the door, then stopped, one hand resting on it. "Hannah?" he asked.

Her eyes met his. "Yes?"

"I didn't answer your question earlier. About if I could protect you." His eyes seemed to pierce her. It caused her to suck in a sharp breath. She wasn't sure why. Was he about to tell her he couldn't? What on earth would she do then?

A long moment passed, then Eli continued, his face made of stone, "No one's going to lay a finger on you while I'm here. I promise you that."

Chapter 6

Hannah yawned as she filled the kettle. She checked on the oats, then stirred them as they started to thicken. She'd had a hard time sleeping last night. For some reason that she couldn't comprehend, Eli's words to her before he left the house kept floating through her mind.

Of course, he'd only said what he should...being a hired gun and all. But the way he'd said it. Fiercely. Protectively. It made her shiver each time she thought about it.

Meg bounded into the kitchen and waited impatiently for her breakfast. Once it was in front of her, she nearly gulped down her oats. "Can I go outside and play in the garden?" she asked.

Hannah nodded. "Go ahead. I'm going to do my washing today, so you can help me in a little while to hang it."

Hugging her mother, Meg skipped out of the house, her doll tucked under her arm. Hannah looked up as Gus and Eli walked in, then quickly filled their bowls with the cooked oats and set out the jug of molasses and a jar of raisins. "Good morning," she said. "Was everything quiet last night?"

Gus nodded and he picked up the molasses. "Nothing unusual."

"Good," Hannah said. She set spoons down on the table and poured cups of coffee for the men.

"I'd like to ride out again around the property," Eli said after a few bites. "I want to go just beyond and see where Wallace's portion of the land starts, and what he's got there."

"I'll go along," Gus told him. "Show you where it is again."

Leaving them to their conversation, Hannah left the kitchen and gathered up her laundry to wash. She slipped outside and looked up as a short time later, she saw Gus and Eli ride away.

Meg was still in the garden, poking at the ground with a stick. Hannah drew water from the well and started scrubbing at the laundry. A half hour later, she called, "Meg! Come help me."

When Meg didn't answer, Hannah stood and went to go find her daughter. "Meg? Did you hear me?" she called, walking to the garden.

A quick glance around showed her Meg wasn't there. She walked to the privy, wondering if she was there, and then to the house. "Meg? Meg!"

There was no answer. A sick feeling grew in Hannah. Something was wrong. Meg wouldn't not answer her. She ran back to the garden, screaming. "Meg! Meg!"

Where could she be? Hannah dashed back into the house. "Meg, if you are playing, this isn't funny," she said, her voice trembling. "You need to come here, right now."

There was still no answer. Hannah hadn't thought there would be. Meg never played tricks. Now fully panicked, Hannah ran out to the barn. Gus's warning about not going anywhere without him played through her mind, but she didn't care. She had to find Meg. With trembling fingers, she unhooked a bridle from the wall. "Come here, girl," she said to the sandy colored mare that was munching grass in the pen.

The mare waited patiently while Hannah put on the bridle, then attached reins. She looked over to where the saddle rested. There was no way she could lift it and put it on. Not in her condition. Really, she shouldn't even be riding.

Leading the horse outside, she took her over to the fence. She'd go bareback, that's what she'd do. It had been a while, but she could manage. Hannah pulled her skirts up with one hand, the other trying to hold the mare steady.

She'd just started to put one foot on the lower rail of the wooden fence to get some height when she heard riders.

"What are you doing?" Gus hollered, panic evident in his face. "Fool woman! Your baby! Get down."

Hannah turned her tear-stained face to him, but obeyed, setting both feet on the ground. She still tightly held the mare, tightly, who sensed her distress.

Gus got off his horse faster than she'd ever seen and took the mare from her. Hannah reached out and grabbed his arm. "Meg's gone! She's gone!" Her voice had a high pitch she didn't recognize.

Eli wheeled sharply atop his horse. "Where was she last?"

"The garden," Hannah sobbed, her panic now full. She pointed, even though Eli knew where the garden was.

Quickly, the gunslinger slid off his horse and ran to the garden. As Gus approached, Eli held up a hand. "Stop. Tracks." He pointed, and Hannah shook her head.

"I don't see anything." Her eyes scanned where he pointed.

"The grass is beaten here. A twig snapped," Eli explained, squatting as he examined the ground. "Gus, stay here. This could be a distraction to hurt Hannah. I'll get Meg." He mounted his large black horse and met Hannah's eyes. "I'll bring her back," he promised.

Before Hannah could blink, Eli was gone, heading in the direction of the creek. Hannah turned to Gus in a panic.

She grabbed at his arm and shook it. "I was right here! I didn't leave her!"

The old man wrapped his arm around her shoulders. "I know, my girl. I know." He shook his fist, his eyes glaring off in the distance. "That no good Wallace Carson. He's behind this, I'm sure."

Hannah didn't say anything. She couldn't. It felt like her heart had been ripped from her. She knew Wallace wasn't above threatening a person. He'd shown that many times, even before Jim had gone. But a child? To abduct and possibly hurt a child?

Gus looked down at her and said, "Now don't you worry. We've got ourselves a gunslinger now. He's the best of the best because he's not just quick on the draw. Remember, he's a dang good tracker too."

"I hope so," Hannah said. She looked at Gus, an overwhelming fear filling her voice. "What if...what if..." She couldn't even say the words. They were too terrible to think.

"Let's go inside," Gus urged. "Don't do no good waiting out here. Just makes you more anxious." He gently guided her toward the house's door. Hannah looked once more over her shoulder, then gasped. Drawing closer, Eli was riding toward them, and in front of him, held carefully in his arms and waving, was Meg.

Hannah picked up her skirts, not caring at all if a little ankle showed, and ran toward the horse. Eli slowed to a walk, and then, coming up beside Hannah, plucked Meg from the saddle as if she was no more than a bit of fluff, and handed her to Gus.

"My baby!" Hannah cried, burying her face into Meg's hair as she leaned in. She breathed her in deeply, then looked up at Eli, her eyes shining with unshed tears. "Thank you."

"Found her by the creek," Eli said. A frown crossed his face. "She hadn't been alone, though. Someone left just as I got there. I wanted to go after them, but I thought it was more important to get her back to you."

"Who do you think it was?" Hannah asked. "Were you able to see what they looked like?"

Eli shook his head, but Meg piped up. "I can tell you that, Mama. It was the man who's going to marry you! Uncle Wallace."

Hannah stiffened. "I'm not marrying him," she said. "Let's get in the house. It's time for dinner."

"But you have to!" Meg protested. She pushed out her lower lip. "He promised me when you did, he'd buy me a candy every Saturday, and I'd get to pick it."

"Your Uncle Wallace is full of promises," Hannah said wryly. "None of the good ones he ever keeps."

Eli dismounted and swung Meg into his arms. "Sweetheart, if that's what it takes to win over your heart, I'll buy you a whole jar of candy tomorrow."

He carried Meg into the house as she giggled, telling him her favorite kind of treats, while Hannah stood in shock.

"Wallace will stoop to anything to get this land," she hissed. "Even kidnapping and bribing a child. A candy every Saturday. I doubt that."

Gus nodded slowly. "Get the land, get you. It might all be one and the same to him now. He doesn't like people standing up to him, and that's what you've done."

"I don't have a choice," Hannah said. She looked at Gus pleadingly. Surely he understood why.

"You don't," he agreed, and ran a hand over his whiskers. "But the fact he was able to sneak up and get Meg? That means we aren't watching close enough. Maybe this time was a warning, and he let her go. Might be next time he don't."

Chapter 7

Hannah wiped a hand across her forehead. It was hot. Too hot for this time of year, but that didn't matter. Chores needed to be done. Meg was with Gus in the barn, close under his watch. Eli was...she wasn't sure where, but Hannah was picking up the cut wood from the pile Gus had chopped, and carrying it, a piece or two at a time, to the woodpile.

Strands of hair clung to her damp face, and she was puffing before long, and stopped to drink deeply from the water bucket.

"You shouldn't be doing this," Eli's voice said, and he stepped close. "Let me."

"You weren't hired to do my chores," Hannah argued, feeling a little guilty as he piled a load into his arms. "Yet somehow, you always turn up when I'm doing them."

It was true. Eli had been there a little over two weeks now. Things had been quiet after Meg's disappearance, and she hadn't been hurt, but she'd also not been out of Hannah or Gus's sight the whole time ever since.

"Sure I was," Eli said, easily lifting the armful of wood. "Protecting you is my job. Protecting you from doing too much is just one of the ways." He winked at her as he stacked the wood. "Besides, we have to make it look realistic if someone is watching. What kind of hired hand would just sit around?"

Hannah stood a moment and bit her lip. "Well...thank you," she said. "It's been hard, without having help around here."

"Did you have hands around the place when your husband was alive?" Eli asked, lifting another load.

It was hard to pull her eyes from the muscles that were rippling under his shirt. What had he asked? Blinking a few times, it came to her and she answered. "We did. Six other men. When Jim died, they all went to work for Wallace. I didn't understand it at the time. They were paid well and fed three meals a day. Treated like family." She shook her head. "I guess that wasn't good enough."

"What's Wallace's problem, anyway?" Eli asked, dropping the armful of wood down at the pile.

"Wallace has always been jealous about the fact that Jim got this portion of land and he didn't."

"This is a smaller plot of land than his," Eli observed. "I noticed that when riding out the first morning. This plot is fifty acres. Gus told me the other is seventy."

"You are right," she said. "But this has better access to water and the soil is more fertile. His is larger, but it also has a lot more rocks in it. I don't know why Jim got this plot of land and his brother didn't. Jim already had the land when we got married, and honestly, I never thought to ask. It didn't really come up in the conversation."

"How many men do you think are on Wallace's land right now?" Eli paused his work and turned to her, his eyes serious.

Hannah pursed her lips as she thought about it. Working the numbers in her head, she finally said, "He runs cattle, so his men are usually doing that, and he's only got one or two around the place with him at any one time. Maybe more if his sons are around."

Eli nodded. "I can handle that many. More if I had to."

He didn't say it boastfully, but matter of fact. He seemed so sure of it, Hannah wondered how many men he'd fought. Gus had convinced him to show off some of his quick draws and threw targets into the air for Eli one afternoon. The gunslinger had hit each of them, much to Gus's delight. Truth be told, she hadn't minded watching either. But still...

"I hope it won't come to that," Hannah said. She grew troubled and met Eli's eyes. "I don't want to cause problems. I just want my son, if he's a son, to have what he deserves. What he's been promised, by right of birth. I'm not trying to make trouble."

"I understand," Eli said. He looked around a moment, his face softening as he took in the house, the barn, and the wide land before them. A small smile formed at the corners of his mouth. "If I were you, I'd want the same." His eyes found their way back to her.

Time seemed to freeze for a moment as they stared at each other. Eli spoke again, his words quiet. "Something beautiful is worth fighting for."

Hannah's mouth suddenly went dry. Her heart started hammering faster than the town blacksmith, and she didn't know what to say. To do. Luckily, he looked back toward the small forest nearby, and waved his hand. "To see this every day, it would be a dream."

"What's it like?" Hannah asked suddenly, in part to clear her mind and in part because she wondered. "Always going from one place to the next?"

Eli considered her words as he gathered more wood. "At first, I liked it," he told her. "When I was younger, it was exciting. I was always seeing something different, going places where danger and adventure were waiting. It was like being the hero in a story."

Hannah smiled. "That's a good way to put it," she said. "You said, though, when you were younger. What about now?"

Eli picked up the water ladle and drank. Wiping his hand across his mouth, he shrugged and dropped the ladle back in the water. "I'm getting tired of it. Don't get me wrong. I'm good at what I do. I've got a lot of money saved up too. But..." he looked again off in the distance, and a touch of wistfulness came into his voice, "I never thought I'd be one to say it, but recently, the idea's been weighing on me. A man eventually wants to settle. Have a family. A wife. A place to hang his hat that's just his."

"Traveling can make that hard," Hannah said.

"Sure can," Eli agreed. He picked up the last of the wood, stacked it, and turned to her. "What do you need me to do next?"

Kiss me. That was the thought that sprang into her mind, and Hannah nearly gasped. She didn't know why she'd think that. Blushing, she answered, "I was going to fix lunch, then get Gus and Meg."

"I'll get them," he promised, and turned.

Hannah watched him walk away. Eli's damp shirt was clinging to his arms and chest, revealing his shape underneath. She let her eyes linger for a moment, then a strange melancholy washed over her. She was enjoying having him around the place. Eli seemed to fill an emptiness she didn't know had been in her. It wasn't just her, but also in Gus and Meg, she told herself. They all felt...complete with him here.

That's what she tried to tell herself, anyway, as she walked into the kitchen and started to slice bread and set out cheese and cold sliced ham. The truth was quite different. She really didn't know what the others thought. But she knew when Eli left, she was going to miss him. And not just because he helped with the chores.

Chapter 8

Gus wandered into the kitchen where Hannah was stirring a pot of beans. After checking on her cornbread, she looked over at him. "I need to go to town today. Do you want to go with me?"

"Gonna storm," he grumbled. "Feel it in my knee."

"Stay here then," Eli said, walking into the room, Meg trailing him. "I'll go. I can hitch up the wagon after we eat."

"Gonna storm," Gus repeated. He shook his head and wagged his finger. "You'll get your supplies wet."

"I'll just have to chance it." Hannah smiled at him, peeking through the kitchen window at the blue sky. "Maybe it will hold a while."

There was no use arguing with Gus about his "weather knee," which was more often wrong than right. She'd learned that very quickly.

"Bring me a candy!" Meg chirped, looking up at Eli pleadingly.

"Meg!" Hannah scolded. "Young ladies don't ask for gifts. That's rude."

Eli winked at the little girl. "I might," he said, "if you'll promise to take good care of Gus and his sore knee."

"I promise," Meg said, bobbing her head up and down.

It was all Hannah could do not to roll her eyes. Somehow, in the short time Eli had been there, Meg had gotten him wrapped around her finger. It had started the day after he arrived. She followed him everywhere he went, and in return, he plied her with stories and sweets, and even some small wooden carved animals he'd made. He was spoiling her, and it was going to make it all the more difficult when he had to leave.

Hannah had told him so one evening, as he sat whittling a fox. Eli had shrugged. "Well then, don't have that baby of yours too soon," he said, pointing to her large stomach.

Near speechless, she had just stared at him. He'd given her that grin he sometimes shared with her, the one where his ice-blue eyes twinkled, and she got a glimpse into the humor his personality had. It had made her laugh.

Looking at Eli sitting with Meg and Gus at the table made Hannah feel that pang of longing again. Right now, everything felt complete. Soon, though, in only a month, he'd likely be leaving. Once her baby was born, she'd know if she needed to leave too. If that was the case, would she ever feel so content again? Eli had effortlessly slid into their lives. He'd made himself valuable, and he'd given friendship to her and Gus, and become a father figure to Meg.

That would all be sorely missed.

But it wasn't something she could think about. Should think about. This was a business transaction. Nothing more.

Hannah dished out the meal and placed it on the table. As Eli took his bowl, his fingers brushed against hers, and she caught her breath. It was hard to deny it. She felt attracted to him. At times, she thought he might feel the same. It was a feeling that had only grown, and though she'd tried very hard to ignore it, it grew unwanted, like weeds in her garden.

She had to stop the feeling, or else her heart might break in two once he left. The thought saddened her each time it came to mind, but there was no way to prevent it, and no way to even dare hope she and Eli could be a pair. He was a gunslinger, with an exciting life filled with wandering and danger. She was simply a mother to one, soon to be two, in a terrible mess, and soon, possibly with nowhere to live.

***

"You sure you want to go today?" Gus asked, pointing to the sky.

"Gonna storm," Meg said solemnly. "My knee says so." She pointed to one knee, then the other.

Hannah fought back a groan. It was Eli who answered, though. "Can't get your candy unless I do, sweetheart. Be good."

At that, Meg's face brightened. "I want—"

"Whatever Mr. Eli is so kind to get you," Hannah said, fixing her daughter with a firm look. "Even if it's nothing."

"Yes, Mama," Meg said, her head lowering, but Hannah didn't miss the wink Eli gave her daughter, and the grin that flashed over Meg's face as she also winked, half her face scrunching.

Gus helped Hannah into the wagon and stepped back. "Don't worry, we're going to be just fine while you're gone. Always chores to do," he said.

The wagon rolled forward, and Hannah waved goodbye. Turning forward again, she said, "Thank you for driving me, Eli. I appreciate it."

"I don't mind. Gives us a chance to talk. I'm curious, too, about seeing a little more of the town. Maybe some of the folk. You can learn a lot about someone just by observing them."

"And what have you observed about us?" Hannah asked curiously.

Eli tipped his hat up a little higher. "A lot, actually."

When he didn't say anything else, Hannah nudged him. "Go on."

He flashed her a grin. "Well, take Gus."

"What about him?"

"He cares a lot for you and Meg. You're the daughter he didn't have. He wishes he could do more, but he's getting up there in years, and he doesn't like it. He's determined to help around the place, and worried about what might happen when he can't. Both to him and to you."

Hannah felt surprised. She'd never realized Gus felt that way. And she'd also never thought about what might happen when Gus couldn't help her. She sighed and rubbed at her forehead. "It's too much," she murmured.

"What is?" Eli asked. His sharp gaze fixed on her.

"I...I didn't mean to speak aloud." Hannah shrugged. "But if you must know, everything. It's all too much. Even if I keep the land for my son, I don't know how we will work it. Gus *is* getting old. It's already too much for the two of us. I might end up losing the land, even if I don't want to.

"Wallace won't let us have any hands to help. I can send away for some, but will they stay? We must have help. And if I do have a son, I'll have to keep my eyes on him constantly. If something were to happen to him, say Wallace harms him or he has an accident, then I'm possibly right back in this position again. Helpless. Hopeless."

Hannah could feel Eli's eyes on her, but she didn't want to look at him. She sat stiffly, willing herself not to get emotional as she stared at her hands tightly balled in her lap.

Taking a deep breath, she looked to the side. The landscape, normally beautiful this time of year, wasn't even enough to distract her. Tiny purple dots in the distance were likely lavender, and she wondered about planting some herself. But just as soon as the thought came, she bitterly realized it was futile.

Maybe she ought to marry Wallace. Her life would be just as miserable with him as trying to be on her own.

However, just as she thought that, a warm, rough hand brushed hers. Hannah's eyes widened as she looked at her lap and saw Eli's hand resting on hers. He gave the softest of squeezes, his eyes still pointed toward the road. She stared at him. His Adam's apple bobbed, and there was a tightness in his eyes.

"Hannah," he said quietly, giving her hand another light squeeze before pulling it away, "you've got me."

A thousand thoughts went through her mind. The first being, but for how long? She couldn't pay him forever. The next was, what would it be like, having Eli with her forever? Meg adored him. Gus enjoyed talking about the old days and adventures with someone who'd done much of the same, and she...she kept each of these moments, each of these words or touches or smiles, deep in her being, eagerly consuming them.

Would he stay? How could she ask him? She longed to know the answer. At the same time, the practical side of her knew a man like him wouldn't want to have a woman like her. She had a child, and another on the way. Men didn't want to take on a woman with children. Then, there was the whole problem of Wallace and the land. She was undesirable.

She had to answer him, though. There was a tenseness from Eli, and Hannah realized she'd not said anything for several long moments. Hesitantly, she reached her hand out, and rested it on his arm. Her chest felt tight, and her hand shook. What was she thinking?

Eli's hand rested on top of hers. A feeling of comfort, of closeness, filled her. Almost without realizing it, Hannah shifted closer, wanting to feel more of him. So close, they were nearly touching on the small seat. Eli looked down at her for a moment, and her pulse raced. There was something in his eyes that made her want to move even closer.

She would have, had she not risked looking wanton. At this moment, she almost didn't care. She was longing for Eli to stay with her, and nearly desperate to tell him to.

"Hannah." His voice was low, almost a deep whisper, and his eyes were burning. His head lowered.

She was about to answer, her own chin lifting slightly, when a movement from the corner of her eye caught her attention.

"Watch out!" she screamed.

Chapter 9

Eli pulled up on the reins as a doe bolted in front of their wagon. The wagon came to a sudden stop, the horses obediently staying calm, and Hannah winced, clutching her stomach as it jolted.

"Are you all right?" Eli asked her, his tone anxious.

"I'm fine," she assured him. "I'm glad the horses didn't trample it."

"Me too. It could have gotten itself tangled up in the harnesses and spooked the horses something fierce." Eli shook his head, and Hannah could have sworn that she saw him blush. "I best keep my eyes on the road."

She laughed, and when they started again, sat a little closer than was necessary, but neither of them said anything, just traded glances under their lashes when they thought the other wasn't looking.

As they rode into town, Hannah reached for her list. She looked it over again, then counted the money in her purse. A twinge of worry struck her. Would Mrs. Stover still sell her the goods she needed?

When the wagon pulled up, Eli jumped out, then helped her down. "I'll park," he said. "Which store? This one?" He pointed to the general store.

"Yes. I'll be in there," Hannah said.

With a nod, he left, and she walked into the shop. Mrs. Stover greeted her with a smile.

"My dear, it's been a while. How are you?" Mrs. Stover eyed her stomach. "Getting closer to time."

"And judgment day," Hannah said, her smile and words tight.

Mrs. Stover gave her a sympathetic look, but didn't say anything. What could she say? They both knew it was true.

"Am I allowed to place an order still?" Hannah asked quietly.

"Of course," Mrs. Stover answered briskly. "Do you have a list?"

Hannah handed it to her, and Mrs. Stover began pulling items off the shelf. The door opened, and Hannah turned to see Eli stride in.

"Hello. Be with you soon," Mrs. Stover said to him.

"It's fine. I'm here with Mrs. Carson," Eli said.

"Oh?" The shopkeepers's eyebrows shot up.

"Yes. Gus managed to find us someone willing to help around the place," Hannah said.

"And a fine-looking one too," Mrs. Stover said, not the least bit embarrassed. Then, she looked at Hannah approvingly. "I'm glad. I don't agree with what Wallace has done. I told you that."

She turned back to the groceries while Eli strolled over to the candies. He looked for a few moments, then wandered back.

"Anything else?" Mrs. Stover asked once everything Hannah had requested was piled near the counter.

"Yes. Let me have a dime's worth of that penny candy and another dime's worth each of lemon drops and peppermint."

"Someone's got a sweet tooth," Mrs. Stover said with a smile, but she pulled out the brown paper and packaged the candies.

"Sure do." Eli winked at her, and Mrs. Stover blushed.

He handed her over the money for the candy and Hannah's groceries. Hannah opened her mouth to object, but he shook his head at her. She didn't want to argue in front of Mrs. Stover, so she nodded.

"Come back anytime," Mrs. Stover said, waving goodbye, her eyes not leaving Eli.

It was silly, but Hannah felt a mixture of pride to be with him, and jealousy that others noticed how fine-looking of a man he was.

Hannah waited in front of the store while Eli carried out the sacks of flour, then returned and carried the rest of the purchases in a large box.

"Let me help you in," Eli said.

Hannah paused as two men rode up on their horses, blocking the wagon. They were an unwelcome sight.

"How are you, Hannah?" Wallace looked down at her. He let his eyes roam over her a long moment, then turned to Eli. "Who's this?"

"This is the man who's been helping around the place. Since you took everyone else who worked for Jim." Hannah stood, her shoulders squared. She'd be darned if she let Wallace ruffle her.

Wallace took in Eli and gave a slow nod. "Wallace Carson. What's your name, son?"

"Eli."

"Eli, huh? You don't want to be working for that woman." He tossed a look at Hannah. "She won't pay you what you're worth. I could use a man like you to help out at my place. I'll pay you triple what she does."

Hannah stiffened. "Triple?"

"A man should be paid what he's worth." Wallace smirked. "Reconsidered my offer, Hannah?"

"No," she said.

Wallace shrugged. "Have it your way. The land will be mine eventually." He looked at Eli, his hard expression turning into one of humor. "When her husband, my brother, died, I offered out of charity to take her in. She's stubborn, though. Would rather see her children starve before accepting an offer of kindness. You watch out. She looks pretty, but she's as black on the inside as they come."

Hannah sensed Eli stiffen, but his voice was casual, curious. "What do you mean?"

She worried for a moment he might be considering Wallace's offer, but she felt his hand brush against the small of her back and relaxed. He was likely playing along. Getting a feel for Wallace and keeping quiet about who he was. It made sense. It made him, and Hannah by default, less of a threat.

"I mean, she's from bad stock. My brother took pity on her when he married her. She didn't bring nothing to the marriage but her good looks. No dowry, nothing. Matter of fact, they were glad to be rid of her."

Wallace leaned in close, and his voice dropped. "Apple don't fall far from the tree. Expect her brats to be the same."

Hannah's eyes blazed, and she stepped forward angrily. A hand on her wrist pulled her back. She shot a glare at Eli.

"Thank you for the offer. I'll consider it," Eli said mildly. "I like to find things out for myself first. But I'll seek you out, Mr. Carson, if I change my mind."

That seemed to satisfy Wallace. He nodded and turned, not even looking at Hannah again. Angrily, Hannah turned to Eli. "Why did you hold me back?"

"What would you have done?" he asked her. "He was on a horse. You are a woman who is heavy with child. You need to be careful. That child," he nodded to her stomach, "determines a large part of your future and Meg's, and you seem to keep forgetting that when it's most important. I know you are able to defend yourself. But there are times you need to let others help you for your own good. This is one of them."

Hannah didn't answer. She couldn't. He was right. Eli helped her into the wagon, and they rolled away from town. Eli reached into the back of the wagon and into one of the packages of candy. The reins in his lap, he pulled open the lemon drops. "Have one," he offered.

Hannah accepted, and they each enjoyed the candy while quietly riding home. She was tired, and the wagon's soft jolts made her doze. Soon, she had slumped against Eli's shoulder. Too tired to care, she lay there. One of his arms moved around her waist, holding her better.

Sleep overcame her until she felt Eli moving his arm and sitting up suddenly. "Are we back?" she asked sleepily. Then, she blinked and frowned. "What time is it?"

The sky had grown alarmingly dark. Before Eli could answer, the sky pelted ice. Hail the size of a thimbles rained down on them. Hannah gasped and shielded her face and head with her arms.

"Hold on," Eli said. "I'm going to try and get us back quick. We're about two miles away."

Hannah nodded and clung to Eli's arm as he urged the horses faster. Around them, the wind blew ferociously. Hannah looked around anxiously for any sign of a tornado, but was relieved not to see one.

"I'll be," Eli muttered. "Gus's knee was right."

Hannah groaned, and gave a small laugh. "He'll never let me hear the end of it," she said as they sped toward the ranch.

He grunted and concentrated. Ahead, Hannah could see the edge of her property. Relief filled her. The sky opened even more, a heavy mixture of hail that soon turned to a downpour.

They'd just gotten onto their property when a bolt of lighting struck. A crackling sound filled her ears, and Hannah looked on in horror as a tree in the yard started to smolder.

Smoke twisted upward, like some sort of snake poised to strike. The way it curled and slithered sent a sickening feeling through her stomach.

Then, the flames started.

Chapter 10

Eli jumped out of the wagon just as Gus burst through the door of the house, a sack in his hand. Hannah scrambled as quickly off the wagon as she could and ran into the house to find more.

Gus beat at the small flames forming while Eli ran to the horses' water trough and filled two buckets. He threw them on the tree, but the rushing wind only flung the water away. Eli ran for more.

Hannah lugged out her bucket of water she kept inside and wet a second sack. She joined Gus, beating at the tree. The fire grew, hot and smoky. Eli rushed up with more water. This time, the flames weakened enough that by redoubling their efforts, Gus and Hannah were able to smother the flames before they grew bigger.

Panting, nearly bent over double with the exertion, Gus gasped out, "I done told you a storm was coming."

Laughing, part in hysterics because she was grateful the fire hadn't spread, and in part because she knew he'd say that, Hannah wrapped her arm around Gus. "So you did," she agreed. "So you did."

"You go on in. I'll help with unloading the wagon," Gus told her.

Not arguing, Hannah went inside and poured herself a mug of cider, the water bucket being empty now. Her throat ached from the smoke, and she was sure she was a mess. A glance down showed soot on her dress.

Eli and Gus came in, setting down the supplies. "Thank you," Hannah said. Outside, the hail seemed to lighten a little, and rain formed, beating against the roof.

"Well, that was exciting," she continued, shaking her head. "Not quite as exciting as the adventures you've had, Eli, but I suspect that's enough excitement for me, anyway."

Eli chuckled. It was warm and tickled her ears. "I'll take rescuing a woman over a gunfight any day."

Hannah flushed and looked away. Eli didn't notice, or if he did, he pretended not to. "I'll get the wagon and the horses up," he said.

"I'll help," Gus started, but Eli shook his head.

"I've got it. You stay in, make sure Hannah doesn't try and lift those heavy sacks."

Gus eyed her and stood up taller. "You would, wouldn't you?" he said in a half scold. "Tell me where you want them."

Eli left, and Hannah rolled her eyes. "I can do things," she said.

"Sure, sure," Gus agreed. "But we've got to keep the young'un safe."

Hannah nodded, and pointed to where she wanted the flour. Gus carried it for her, then came back.

"Trip to town go all right?" he asked.

"We saw Wallace," Hannah said with a grimace. "He tried to hire Eli. He," she stopped, and then spoke softly to her shoes, "didn't speak highly of me."

Gus made to spit, then seemed to remember he was inside. "Don't you worry none. Eli isn't going anywhere."

"Triple, Gus! He offered triple. No wonder we can't get help."

With one wrinkled hand rubbing at his jaw, Gus nodded slowly. "That does make it hard. But now we know how much he's offering the ones he don't threaten."

Hannah nodded and sighed.

"Something else bothering you?" Gus asked, his blue eyes sharp as he stared at her. "I reckon I can tell by now."

Hannah laughed. "No, it's nothing."

"Go on. What's this nothing you aren't telling me?"

Her lips twisted into a smile. Gus loved gossip as much as anyone, and his eyes were bright. Should she really tell him what she was thinking? She shrugged. She guessed it didn't matter.

"Fine. Eli..." She stopped and blushed again. "Eli held my hand for a moment on the ride. Sometimes, I think I see him staring at me."

"Well, sure," Gus agreed. "He's a man, ain't he? And you're a good-looking widow. Ain't nothing wrong with that." He raised his eyebrows at her. "You could do a lot worse. Why don't you try and catch him?"

"Gus!" Hannah gasped. "What kind of woman do you think I am?"

The old man shrugged. "One who needs a push to get herself a man who'll look after her."

Hannah put her hands on her hips. "I'm just fine, thank you. Besides, I have you."

It was Gus's turn to blush, and he mumbled something down at his boots that she couldn't quite make out.

"What was that?"

"I said, I reckon you do. For now, anyway. My girl, what are you going to do, though, when I'm not here to help? Or if you decide I'm not able to help, and I become nothing but a burden in my old age?"

Hannah shook her head. "You'll never be a burden. You are my family. And if you weren't here, I wouldn't know what to do." She leaned forward and kissed his weathered cheek. "Don't you be going anywhere. I won't have it," she scolded, and turned away quickly as she saw him tearing up.

Meg was in the kitchen, eying the brown paper packages that were tied with white string. "What's that, Mama?"

"Those are Eli's," Hannah said.

Her eyes round, Meg stared at them until Eli came through the door. He'd changed from his smoky clothes, but he was damp from the rain. "Apologies for dripping," he said, standing close to the stove. "I just wanted to check and make sure you were all right."

"Just fine," Hannah said, and smiled at him. "Thank you for your help. Taking me to town, carrying everything, putting out the fire."

"It was scary," Meg said. "My doll wanted to hide, so we went under the bed, Mama."

Eli came over to her. "I have just the thing for you and your doll," he said. "A reward for being so brave."

Meg watched as he opened one of the packages and pulled out some of the penny candy. Placing a handful of it into a jar, he pushed it to her. "There. That's all for you and your doll. But you can only eat it when your mama tells you that you can. Understand?"

Meg's eyes were wide. Hannah knew she'd never seen so many sweets before, except for in the store. Meg jumped up and flung herself at Eli. "Thank you," she said, and started crying.

Eli leaned down and picked her up. "Sweetheart, why are you crying?"

Burying her head into his neck, Meg sniffled, "Because I like you. Even if you don't give me candy, and I don't want you to ever go away."

Eli held her tightly, and his eyes met Hannah's over Meg's head. Hannah's eyes felt misty, and she gave a small smile, and turned to the stove, preparing to get the evening meal started. She felt just the same as Meg did, only she couldn't say it. It wasn't proper.

"I'm not going anywhere any time soon," Eli promised. "Now, you pick out a candy, and you and your doll go share it. I want to talk with Mr. Gus."

Meg nodded, took a long time choosing, then picked out an orange colored candy and skipped out of the room.

Gus sat at the table. "You're spoiling her."

Hannah laughed. "He bought more than he gave her."

"I like candy." Eli grinned. "Always have, so I understand her perfectly." He opened the other bundles. "Want a piece?" he offered.

"I'm fine," Hannah said with a smile, but Gus helped himself to a peppermint.

"You wanted to talk to me?" he asked.

"I do," Eli said, taking a seat at the table. He wrapped the packages up. "I'll keep this in the bunkhouse. Help yourself though, Gus." At the old man's nod, he continued. "We ran into Wallace today."

"Hannah mentioned that," Gus answered.

"What neither of you knows, is that before I came into the store, I overheard him talking to the man he was with. I couldn't hear all of it, but he said it was past time to 'remove the problem.'"

Hannah spun, worry filling her. She tried to speak, but her mouth felt like it was full of cotton. The look traded between Eli and Gus didn't escape her. Trembling, and pressing her hands tightly into each other, she tried again. "Remove the problem? Does that mean...me?"

Chapter 11

Gus smacked the table. "Can't stand that man," he growled.

"We can't jump to conclusions, but I'm wondering if we should get a little more backup. Call the local sheriff."

"Can't do it," Gus said, and shook his head.

"Why not?" Eli asked.

"The sheriff is Wallace's uncle. The deputy is his son-in-law." Hannah pressed her lips together. "They aren't going to help. And they'll keep any other lawmen nearby from helping too."

Eli frowned. He was quiet a moment, and Hannah could tell he was thinking. He drummed his fingers on the table. "What about some extra help around the ranch, if you get my meaning," Eli suggested. "I feel confident in taking care of things the way they stand, but I'm not a fool.

If Wallace and his men greatly outnumbered us, well then, I don't want to get into a position where I have to choose who to protect."

He didn't say it, but his eyes traveled to the room where Meg was, and down to Hannah's stomach, then her face. Hannah knew she was pale. It certainly felt like all the blood had rushed from her head.

"What are you suggesting?" she asked. "Seeing if anyone will come on as hands?"

At the same time, Gus shook his head. "Ain't nobody in town who will help. Not a one. Just told you that."

Eli frowned. "Do you mean every man in town is either in his pocket or being threatened by him? Every man?"

"That's right," Gus said. "I wasn't lying when I told you that when you first got here. He's a real influential man one way or another."

"I have every right to be here on this land until my child is born," Hannah said, but the fight wasn't in her words. Instead, a feeling of dread overcame her. Hannah hoped he wouldn't, but Eli spoke aloud the very question she asked herself and she hated.

"What if it is a son?" Eli asked. His tone wasn't cold or judgmental, it was one of concern. One of fact. "If your child inherits the land, how are you going to take care of it? Even more importantly, do you really think that Wallace is going to back down? Do you think that he is going to just go away and leave you and your son alone?"

Hannah bit down on her lip. The law was on her side! But the way Eli said it made her realize that perhaps she was very, very wrong to even hope that a man like Wallace would obey it, especially since there weren't many out there Wallace didn't bully around or bribe.

Judging by the look on Gus's face, he felt the same. When she realized Eli was still staring at her, she looked away for a moment, then back at him with a sigh. "I suppose I thought he would."

"That's why I think we need a few more men," Eli told her. "One way or another, judgment day is coming. You're going to have to fight to protect yourself and your children, and you need people to help you."

"I got a little money," Gus started.

"No," Hannah said firmly. She turned to Eli. "We have enough to pay you, but no more." Tears filled her eyes. "Jim didn't have much but the land. And his plans for it, to grow wealth, were cut short. It took most of what we had to keep going after he passed."

"There's no family who can help you? Take you in?" Eli asked.

"I don't have any," Hannah admitted. "Maybe that's part of why Wallace doesn't like me. I'm not from here originally. As a matter of fact, my parents were dirt poor. We didn't have two coins to rub together growing up. One night, my father left in the middle of the night and didn't come back. I wasn't too much older than Meg when that happened. My mother got remarried about a year later, but she caught sick when I was a teenager. After she passed away, and I was of age, my stepfather wasn't interested in supporting me any further. I became a schoolteacher out this way, and that's where I met Jim. He was on the school board. We started courting and got married a little while later."

"What she's not saying," Gus added, "was that she didn't get much say in that marriage. Weren't enough children in the school. They was going to shut it down, and she couldn't find another position."

Hannah tersely replied, "I'd have found something."

"Sure would'a," Gus agreed, "but Jim begged her to stay. Needed a cook for his men. Was gonna hire her as that, then decided he'd rather just have her as his wife. Wouldn't have to pay her that way."

Pursing her lips, Hannah folded her arms. "That's enough, old man."

"Now, had a man like you come along—" Gus began.

"That's enough," Hannah snapped, and glared at him. "If you aren't going to be helpful, get out of my kitchen. I might not have it much longer, but while I do, it's mine, and I can have in it who I please."

Gus just smirked at her, and Hannah's face felt like it was nearly on fire. Eli just watched, amusement in his eyes. He was the first to break the silence. "It sounds like local men are out. Same with any in the nearby towns. I've got a few favors I can call in," he said, and then quickly raised a hand, looking at Hannah. "It won't cost a nickel. Just some food for the men and a place to stay."

"That I can do," she said. "But you trust them?"

The look that came over Eli's face near chilled her. His reply was much worse.

"Better than that. I don't trust them one bit."

Chapter 12

Hannah scrubbed at the wash in her tub, making sure to keep an eye on Meg, who was poking at a cricket with a stick, trying to get it to climb on so she could carry it around to a little box she'd found. Within a few days of Eli sending messages to the men he knew, they'd shown up. Today, she finally insisted that they let her wash their clothes. There was no reason she couldn't do that, not when they were doing so much for her.

Gavin was chopping wood. The steady twack, clunk, twack, clunk rhythm was faster than she'd ever heard. He'd only been at it for a day, and already had a large pile beside him. Gavin was quiet, with dark hair, nearly a jet-black, and a serious expression she'd only seen him without once, and that was when she'd brought out a peach pie. Then, his eyes widened, and he'd nearly put away half of it on his own. She'd need to get some more peaches to make him another.

Near the barn, Billy was stacking hay and feed for the horses. His muscles bulged with each heavy sack he threw, then stacked. The opposite of either Gavin or Eli, Billy was blond, with hair so pale it could be almost mistaken for white. Always with a smile on his face, or a whistle coming out of his lips, he was the more sociable of the men. He was one of four and told her he'd grown up on a ranch himself, so was no stranger to chores. He also admitted that's why he got out of there as soon as he could. It was more work than he wanted to do.

Neither of the men shared how they knew Eli, and Eli hadn't explained it either. Each time Hannah thought she might ask, she reconsidered. It likely wasn't something she wanted to know. If Eli was a gunslinger, it was quite a good bet these men were as well...or even something more dangerous. Eli assured her they'd protect her and Meg, and that was all that mattered.

They'd been there a week now, and Hannah had provided all they needed for the bunkhouse and their meals. Eli and Gus had shown them around, taking them around the property and even pointing out Wallace's land.

Wallace had been quiet after he'd taken Meg. Hannah didn't doubt for a minute, though, that he wasn't giving up on the land. The way the lawyer had explained it, was Wallace and Jim's father had left the land equally to his boys, and it was divided the way it had been staked. Since Wallace had sons, his would eventually go to them, and they could either split it among themselves or work it together.

Jim's land, in order to stay his or his family's, would need to be passed down to a son. That's why Wallace wanted it so badly. If Jim were alive, he'd have many more years to try for a son. Without one, Wallace got another fifty acres for his two boys, effectively not reducing their landholdings at all.

But there was still a chance, Hannah thought, stopping to rest a moment as the babe inside her kicked. "It won't be much longer," she promised it.

And son or daughter, I'll care for you. No matter what I have to do or where I have to go.

Her eyes searched for Eli. As much as she welcomed the extra protection and the help, that meant she had less time just with Eli. There had only been a few lingering looks, brushes of his hand against hers, and one moment where they'd stared at each other so intently, Hannah was sure he'd kiss her.

But he didn't.

Gus had strolled in and asked for Eli's help with something, and disappointed, she'd turned and resumed what it was she'd been doing.

Hannah stretched her back for a moment, then started to wring the shirts. The wet pile grew beside her until at last everything was wrung. Carrying the laundry over to the line between two trees, she hung them out, then frowned as a dust cloud in the distance formed.

She wasn't the only one who noticed it. Gavin let out a strange whistle, and Billy, still near the barn, answered with one the same, as did Eli from the rear of the house. Billy appeared by the woodpile as if he'd been there the whole time and slowly started to stack.

Eli came from around the back of the house, a water-filled bucket in hand, while Gus sat up from his spot on the porch and ran a stone over a knife, sharpening it.

Each of the men were ready for whoever the visitor was, and Hannah was amazed. If she hadn't known any better, she'd have just thought they were ranch hands, busy at work.

Eli had warned them not to give away who they were, and Billy had complained that he'd worked too hard on his reputation not to use it when needed, but he'd agreed, quieted by a look from Eli.

The rider drew closer, and Hannah saw it was Wallace, along with his oldest son Jethro. She closed her eyes for a moment, willing strength to fill her. Like a terrible omen, a cloud covered the bright sun for a moment, turning the skies gray.

Wallace came to a stop and looked down at her. She held her breath, waiting for him to speak, but he jumped down, his son doing the same, and they walked over to Gavin and Billy at the woodpile.

"New hands, huh?" Wallace said. He nodded at them. "Wallace Carson. Could use a few more men at my place. Pay's better," he said.

Billy straightened and ran a sleeve across his forehead, as if he was considering. "Nah," he finally answered. "Just got here. I like it good enough."

"Same," Gavin said.

"Figures," Wallace sneered. He looked over at Hannah. "You set a bad example for your daughter. An unmarried woman, living with four men."

"I'm not living with anyone," Hannah retorted, "except for my daughter and unborn child. My hired help sleeps in the bunkhouse, under the watchful eye of Gus, who is a man held in high regard."

"Doesn't matter the truth." Wallace shrugged. "You know that. People will think what they want to think."

"Or what you tell them. Is that it?" Hannah fired back. Her hands were clenched, and anger simmered in her.

"I only want to help you," Wallace said. He opened his hands in a pleading gesture and looked over at the men. "Do you hear her? It's no wonder she doesn't have a man wanting to take her in. A temper like a firecracker. She likes to argue. A man don't want that. He wants a quiet wife."

Seeing he had their attention, he continued, "I've been trying to help her ever since my brother died, but she just refuses." He shook his head sadly. "I'm not lying about her reputation. Word's getting around, and you gentlemen might find yourselves having trouble getting work because of it, once this land is mine."

Gavin's stony face didn't flicker. "I'll take my chances," he said, his voice low.

Wallace's eyes flicked to Billy, who shook his head. "What about you?" he asked Eli. "Considered my offer?"

"I have," Eli said, his tone pleasant. "I like the view on this side of the pasture better."

Gus snorted when he felt Wallace's eyes fall on him, and spit.

With a shrug, Wallace walked back to his horse. "Well, you all remember that. I gave you a chance. What about you, Hannah? My last offer. Marry me. Stop this foolishness. Think of your children."

"I am thinking of my children," Hannah told him. "I'll never marry you, Wallace. No matter how many times you ask me."

He laughed then, a low, deep chuckle that only grew, until he was slapping his thigh, nearly bent over. When he got control of himself, he stood up, a smile stretched from one ear to the next.

"So you say," he said. "But you'll be begging me to take you for my wife soon."

Before she could reply, he'd turned and was on his horse, his oldest son climbing on his. Neither looked back as they rode away.

Hannah stood there, trembling. Then, she felt a terrible pain in her midsection and doubled over, crying out.

Chapter 13

"I'm fine," Hannah protested as Gus pointed to a rocking chair. "It's too early for me to be sitting. Dinner needs fixing."

Gus didn't answer. He just pointed again. Eli walked up to her and put his hands on her shoulders. "Sit. Billy and I will cook. You rest."

"But I'm fine," Hannah sighed as she gave in and sat, picking up a shirt to mend. "The midwife said it's not time yet. Just early pains."

"Hannah." Eli knelt down, and got close enough for her to see the golden flecks in his eyes. Once again, she thought they were absolutely mesmerizing. "I can't take care of you and your baby if you won't let me. Stay here. Sit. Sew if you have to, but that's why we are here. To take care of you."

She wanted to protest. To argue that she was perfectly capable. But a small part of her liked him fussing over her. Taking care of her. Jim hadn't been that way, and she'd always done so much to care for him and the house. To have the luxury of someone to care for her and to help around the property without her having to ask all the time felt...nice.

Reluctantly, Hannah nodded. Eli and Billy went into the house. Gus walked Meg with him to the barn to feed the horses, and Gavin joined her on the porch. He sat and stared at the door to the house for a moment before turning to her.

"I never understood why some men would want to settle down," he said. "But I think I'm seeing why Eli wants to."

"Do you think he ever might?" Hannah asked.

His dark eyes, almost as black as his hair, met hers. "Maybe you've not noticed," he shrugged, "but I have. When you've known someone as long as we've known each other, you see things."

Gavin tipped his chair back against the porch and set his revolver on a small table. "I don't blame him. You've a nice place here, and you're good company."

Hannah's cheeks heated. "Now wait a minute. You can't think—"

"I don't think anything improper," Gavin said mildly. "But I can tell you two like each other."

Her mouth fell open, and she sputtered, searching for the words to deny it. Gavin just shrugged. "I don't care. Honestly," he paused for a long moment, "if you ask me, I think you two are good together. Seeing you, seeing this," he gestured around him, much as Eli had when he first came, "it makes a man want more than the life he's living."

Hannah looked at him for a long moment. His eyes seemed haunted. Was it because of his past? Of a love unrequited or lost? The West wasn't an easy place to live. Sickness, not enough doctors, or the proper kind, dangerous conditions...it was almost endless the ways a life could be ended early. One had to make the most of what time they had. Jim's loss had shown that.

As if he realized she was looking at him, Gavin turned, and gave her a small smile. "Don't go feeling sorry for me," he said. "I've lived a life many would envy. Excitement. Adventure." He grinned at her now. "More money than I'll ever be able to spend, and pretty girls whenever I want them."

"But those things...they aren't enough anymore?" Hannah asked.

Gavin's expression grew thoughtful. "I'm not sure. But I'm not letting that bother me right now. One day at a time. I'm enjoying this job. There's something good feeling about helping out."

"I appreciate you coming," Hannah said. "Wallace scares me."

"He should," Gavin said.

"Gavin," Eli said from the doorway. He shook his head.

Hannah felt her chest tighten. "You aren't telling me something," she said, searching Eli's stony face.

He didn't say anything, and the worried feeling grew. Her eyes sought Gavin's, but he was looking away.

What was it they weren't telling her?

Chapter 14

"We aren't not telling you anything," Eli assured her. He took a seat on the porch, on Meg's stool. "It's just a feeling is all."

"Like something crawling on my neck," Gavin muttered. "He's up to something. Just don't know what it is yet."

"I suspect he doesn't know what it is," Eli mused. "Seeing as he keeps offering Hannah a chance to change her mind. He may be trying to buy time."

"Well, I won't change it," Hannah said. "He can ask me until he's blue in the face. I'm not marrying him."

"Got to do something," Gavin said, not looking up from where he was inspecting his fingernails. "And though I've never asked a woman to marry me, I have to say, threatening doesn't seem like it's a good way to go about it."

Hannah laughed. "I agree," she said. "I can't imagine any girl saying yes to that. Not willingly, anyway," she added.

"I'm glad we're here," Gavin said suddenly. "Never had a job like this before. It's good having something new."

"And that's what we'll be having for dinner," Eli said. "Billy said it's something new he learned to make in Colorado from a"—he stopped himself, looked at Hannah, and then cleared his throat—"well, nevermind."

"I won't ask for any more details," Hannah said, smiling. "It'll be nice to have a meal I didn't cook."

"You might think that." Gavin nodded. "But with Billy, who can tell? Might be good, might not be."

The door opened, and Billy stuck his head out. "Wait till you try this," he said.

They went inside, and Hannah's eyes widened at the dish.

"Dumplings," Billy said proudly. "Made them myself. And...I put raisins in them."

Eli and Billy traded looks while Hannah held back a smile. The smile stayed on her face the rest of the evening, until she fell asleep.

She hadn't been sleeping for long when a sharp pain woke her up. Hannah tried to ignore it, too tired to stand, but it persisted. With a small groan, she rolled out of bed and paced. Was it the baby? Was the midwife wrong?

Opening the door to her room, she wandered into the kitchen and lit the lamp. Maybe a drink would help. The kettle still had water, so she put it on and waited.

Another sharp pain, and this one had her nearly doubled over. She was just fumbling for a chair when the door opened, and Billy came in.

"Saw the light," he said. "I'm on watch. What's happening?"

Hannah couldn't answer. She was in too much pain. Billy frowned, then ran out the door, calling as he went, "Baby's coming!"

***

Hannah struggled to raise her head. She felt weak. It hadn't been this way with Meg. Could it be the stress of her current situation that made this birth harder?

It had been hours. Maybe even days. She wasn't sure at this point. Time had lost all meaning. She just knew pain. Pain and fear. She couldn't take much more.

The midwife had talked soothingly to her, but had also left several times. She wasn't sure where. It had been a long, slow labor. At one point, the doctor had come. She wanted to greet him, but it was all she could do to stay alert.

Hannah was so tired. So weary. *God, please, protect my baby,* she prayed. It was the only thought she could think. *Protect my baby.*

Voices seemed to come from so far away. Sleep was all Hannah wanted. Rest. Just for a while.

There was a cry. A baby? Her baby? Hannah focused. Yes. Her baby.

"One more push," the midwife said.

Hannah did, and the cries continued. Healthy sounds. She sighed, and fell back, sleep claiming her at last.

She wasn't sure how long she slept, but when she woke, the midwife slipped a blanket-wrapped bundle into her arm. Hannah smiled down at her baby.

The midwife left, promising to stop back again tomorrow, and she felt exhausted. She was also thirsty, but the mug seemed so far away.

Her eyes were heavy. Eli slipped into the room. "How are you feeling?" he asked.

"Tired," she whispered. "Thirsty."

He nodded, and held the mug of tea to her lips. She drank, then leaned back into the pillows.

Hannah searched his face. "How long can we keep it a secret, do you think?" she asked.

He shook his head. "Not long. The midwife is sure to tell someone."

"Wallace, you mean." Hannah closed her eyes. She was too tired to think right now. Tomorrow would come soon enough.

"Just sleep," Eli said soothingly.

And she did. For nearly a day, Hannah slept. When she woke, she could hear voices in the main room.

"...then I turned around. Faster than a striking snake, BAM!" Gus's voice rose slightly.

"Would have liked to see that one," Gavin said.

"Reminds me of that time when we fought Rattlesnake," Billy interjected. "Gus, too bad we didn't have someone like you with us."

Hannah smiled. She imagined Gus felt flattered. She struggled to sit, and almost as if he knew she was awake, Eli cracked the door open, and stuck his head in.

"Get you anything?" he asked.

"No, I just need to feed the baby," she said.

Eli peered at the small bundle she held. "Babies are always so red at first," he remarked. "This one is no different."

"They grow out of it quickly," Hannah said, kissing the downy head. Her baby had been born with a full head of hair. She hoped it would stay.

"Thought of a name?" he asked, letting one of his fingers reach toward the baby's tiny hand.

"I have," she said. "I was thinking maybe Benjamin. Ben for short."

"A strong name," Eli said approvingly.

There was a tap at the door, and Billy called, "Can we come in?"

When Hannah nodded, the men, Meg in Gus's arms, came in to see the baby. There were coos and whispers and grins all around.

Meg kissed her brother, then asked, "Mama, does this mean Uncle Wallace will let us stay?"

Time slowed for Hannah. Slowly, she answered, "I don't know, Meg. I don't know."

Chapter 15

"Wallace knows you had the baby," Gus said, out of breath as he walked in the house. He wheezed, leaning forward as he caught his breath. "I was at the blacksmith when he asked me what you named it."

Hannah's first reaction was to look at her baby, nestled in a small bed in the corner of the kitchen. Her next was to groan and sink into a chair. "I guess it's been a week. Too much to ask for a little more time."

"Midwife's his cousin," Gus agreed. "And I sure wouldn't put it past Wallace to sniff around."

Her face brightened then, as a hopeful thought formed. "If he knows, does that mean he realizes the land belongs to Ben? And is going to leave us alone?"

"I don't think so," Gavin answered, from where he leaned against the door.

"Why not?" Hannah asked.

"Because he's riding up now. With the sheriff and a few other men," Billy said.

"But...why?" Hannah asked, incredulously.

"Don't know. Stay inside," Gavin said. "Eli's already in the yard."

Hannah shook her head. "I can't," she said. "If you are my hands, they won't believe you speak for me."

There was a moment of silence, then Gus nodded reluctantly. "She's right."

"There's only six of them," Gavin said, his low voice nearly growling. "I can take out four before they get any closer."

"And leave nothing for me or Eli?" Billy argued.

"Or me?" Gus asked.

If it weren't such a serious moment, Hannah might have given a small laugh. Gus had taken to wearing his old gunbelt, though it was empty. Enamored by the men, Meg had asked for one as well.

The dust came before the riders. With a sigh, Hannah pushed herself up from the chair. "Meg, please stay with your brother," she said.

"I'll stay too," Gavin said. "I've a good spot to shoot from at this window."

"I hope it won't come to that," Hannah said, trying to ignore the glint in his eye, "but thank you."

He nodded, his gaze fixed on the riders.

Gus joined Hannah on the porch. Billy and Gavin pretended to work. Eli at the woodpile, the axe in his hand, Billy with a hammer and some nails near the side of the house as he worked on "fixing" a bench.

Wallace and the sheriff led the riders. Hannah stood silently as they pulled up. She didn't like the expression on his face.

"Here to claim my land," Wallace said loudly.

"You're not here to claim nothing," Gus retorted. "She done have a boy. It's Jim's son, so it's his land now." He didn't even try to keep the smug expression from his voice.

"That's not what I hear," the sheriff said. He tried, and failed, to look sympathetic. "I understand the baby doesn't look like Jim."

Hannah stared at him, stunned. "He's a baby."

"Not good enough," Wallace said with a smile. "Mighty convenient of you, having a boy."

This time, Hannah had to laugh at the ridiculousness of it all. "I had a fifty-fifty chance," she said dryly.

"Midwife said he didn't look anything like Jim. That's enough for me," Wallace said. He shrugged. "Got the law on my side. I'm not heartless, though, Hannah. You can leave tomorrow. Don't have to be today."

Hannah stared between Wallace and the sheriff. Behind her, she could sense the gunslingers focused on the conversation. Anger filled her, and she took a step forward.

"I'm not leaving. I have every right to be here. My lawyer—"

"Will agree with me." Wallace smiled. "I'll see to it."

"Pa, maybe we should just—"

"Quiet, boy. I didn't bring you along to go against my word," Wallace snarled at his oldest son, Jethro.

Hannah's eyes flicked to Jethro for a moment. She wondered what he had been about to say. Was it possible he was on her side or knew something that could help?

"I'm not leaving," she said again, firmly. "Mr. Carson, get off my land." When he started to speak, she raised her voice. "It is my land because I am speaking for my son. The circuit judge comes around soon. He'll agree with me. I have all the papers saying so, and plenty of witnesses."

Wallace leaned forward, and hissed low, "That won't do you no good if you're dead."

"You're threatening me? In front of the sheriff?" Hannah glanced at the sheriff.

"Didn't hear anything," the sheriff said.

"Of course not. I thought family always stuck together. Convenient of you to forget this baby is your nephew." Hannah crossed her arms. "You could have mentored him. Helped him. Instead, you've shown just what kind of a man you are. Threatening and chasing out your own flesh and blood."

Hannah knew she'd said too much. It wasn't even half of what she wanted to say, but Wallace's face turned an angry red, and he started toward her, raising his fist. Gus stepped in front of her, his chest puffed out.

"Want to hit someone?" he shouted. "Go ahead. But it won't be her."

Eli and Billy had moved close at some point, Hannah wasn't sure when, and had moved alongside of her as well. Hannah took a step backward, but she could still observe everything.

Gus was angry looking. His white hair was near standing up on top of his head. Billy wore a smile, one of pure amusement. But Eli...Eli had a face of pure stone. She wondered what Gavin looked like inside of the house.

"Out of my way, boy," Wallace said, looking at Eli.

"I'm not a boy," the gunslinger said. With a smile as cold and as deadly as a rattlesnake, he added, "I'm Eli Jones."

"So?" Wallace scoffed. "That don't mean nothing to me."

"Billy Madison," Billy said quietly, resting a hand at his hip. "And Gavin Jefferson is inside the house."

Wallace's mouth opened, but the sheriff grabbed his arm. "Don't be a fool," he hissed. "You want to walk away?"

"Yeah," Billy mocked. "You want to walk away?"

Jethro started shaking in his saddle. "Pa, we'd better get out of here," he said.

Wallace turned to his son with a sneer, then glared at the sheriff. "What's wrong with you all?" he asked.

"They're smart, that's what," Eli said. His smile grew. "Much smarter than you, Mr. Carson."

Gus was smiling now as well. "That's right," he said, and spat at Wallace's feet. "We got ourselves three of the finest gunslingers around. Read the papers, Carson? You'll see all about them. If you know your letters, that is. Let's see you try and take this land now."

Angrily, Wallace got on his horse. "This isn't over," he hissed.

"It never is, with you," Hannah said tiredly. "I'll see you when the circuit judge comes to town in a few weeks."

"Oh no," Wallace said. "It will be much sooner than that. Gunslingers or not, nothing's going to keep me from what I want."

Chapter 16

"Well, that went well," Gavin said, his voice dry.

"Could have gone better," Gus grumbled. "Would have been better if he'd have wet himself when he heard who you were."

Eli clapped his hand on Gus's shoulder. "The sheriff near did," he assured. "That's good enough for me." He leaned in. "Wouldn't have been the same without you. I'm glad you're here with us."

Gus straightened and grinned. "I do hold my own," he agreed.

Hannah shook her head. "I'm tired of this. I'm tired of Wallace. I'm tired of his threats. I just wish he'd go away."

"Not going to happen," Gus said. "Worse than a gnat in the summer."

"Things are coming to a head," Eli said, not looking up from where he carved a small wooden owl. "It's only a matter of time. He knows who we are now."

"And it's not enough to scare him off?" Hannah asked.

"Not a man as proud as that," Billy said. "He's embarrassed now, and men like him don't like that."

"How long do you think we have before he tries something else?" Hannah asked.

Eli traded looks with the other men, then shrugged. "Don't know. But I can tell you, Gus has his knee, I have the hairs on the back of my neck, and they've not sat down since he rode up."

"Funny thing about Jethro," Gus mumbled around a bite of pie. "He right seemed uncomfortable. Scrap of decency in him, I suspect. Always did take after his ma."

"A lot of good that does," Hannah said. "It's not Jethro who we are dealing with."

At the exact moment the words left her mouth, there was a knock on the door. The gunslingers had their revolvers in hand before Hannah could even blink. Gus rose, and opened the door a crack.

"I've come to warn you," a voice said through the crack.

Gus opened the door wider. "Jethro? What are you doing here? Your pa sent you?" He looked suspicious. Eli went to stand next to him.

Jethro stood, his hat in his hands and his face beaded with sweat. "No, Gus. Honest. Swear on my ma's grave. But Pa's real mad. He's coming tonight."

"Tonight? To do what?" Eli asked. "And why should we trust you?" His tone was cool, and his face expressionless.

Swallowing hard, Jethro looked at Hannah. "I never had no quarrel with you, Hannah. You've always treated me right nice. Like..." he looked down at his boots, took a breath, and looked up, "like my ma did. You don't have to believe me, but I don't want no harm to come to you or Meg or the baby. Pa's gone too far. Claude and I don't even want more land. That's all Pa."

Hannah searched Jethro's face. She sensed he was telling the truth. She nodded. "I know," she answered him quietly. "I don't blame you for any of this, Jethro. Nor your brother, Claude."

A look of relief washed over his face.

"What's he planning?" Eli asked. "Do you know?"

"He didn't let me in on the planning," Jethro said, and he looked angry for a moment. "Doesn't trust me. Says I'm too soft, like Ma was. All I know is he's coming with four other men. They are going to make a distraction, then another, and then come to the house."

"Anything else?" Gus asked. "And don't you be lying to me, boy. You swore on your ma's grave."

"No, sir." Jethro twisted his hat in his hands. "I've got to go, before he finds out I'm gone."

Eli nodded. "Go. But I'd better not find you here tonight when they come."

"You won't," Jethro said. He turned, then turned back, looking over his shoulder. Looking nervous, he asked, "Is it true what they say about you, and Westover Ridge?"

A slow smile spread over Eli's face. "Sure is," he said.

Jethro's expression turned to one of awe, and he left. Hannah asked, "What happened at Westover Ridge?"

"That's not for ladies to know," Gus replied. "But it was one of his finest moments. Took down twenty raiders." The hero worship was evident in his voice.

"It was eighteen." Eli shrugged.

"Close enough," Gus said.

Hannah stood from the table. "Well, I guess we need to get ready, then. They've got their plan. We need one of our own." She stared at Gus, and then each of the gunslingers expectantly. "What should we do?"

Chapter 17

Hannah couldn't seem to stop pacing. She felt restless and scared. If Jethro had been telling the truth, what was going to happen?

She went into the kitchen. Eli sat at the table, with his eyes fastened on the window. His head didn't turn as he asked, "The kids okay?"

Hannah nodded, then realized he likely couldn't see. "Yes," she answered. "They are fine."

She stood watching him for a moment, then poured herself some water from the kettle and dropped in some tea leaves. As she watched them swirl and release their fragrance, she breathed in deeply.

"You should sleep some," Eli said softly.

It was true. She should. It was late at night, but she couldn't. She didn't want to tell him why, but the words slipped out. "How can I sleep, when you and the others are risking your lives for me?"

Eli shot her a quick glance before looking through the window again. "It's—"

"If you are going to say it's your job," Hannah said, her voice trembling, "I don't want to hear it. You've been here for several months now. I...I'd like to think I'm more than a client."

But more in what way, she didn't say. Eli had been nothing but well mannered. Other than when he'd held her hand in the wagon, they hadn't really been alone. She longed for that, desperately wanted to know if he felt for her even a small bit of what she thought she was feeling for him.

Yet each time she let herself wonder, her mind shut down again, reminding her she was a mother of two, and he was a gunslinger, always seeking his next adventure. He wouldn't want to trade his freedom for being settled down with her. When he and the others traded stories, he always looked so happy, so full of...she wasn't sure what, but it sure wasn't full of longing to be a rancher or a farmer or the husband of a widow with two children, no matter how much they—all of them—doted on him.

"That's not what I was going to say," Eli said softly. "I—"

A low whistle came, and Billy walked in. "Switch," he said.

Eli stood and walked to the door. "Step outside with me?" he asked her.

With a nod, Hannah followed him, and Eli took up the post where Billy had been, the corner of the house that allowed a good view of the garden, the barn, and off a ways where the creek was.

They were quiet a moment, then Hannah asked, summoning her courage, "What were you going to say a moment ago?"

In the darkness—the gunslingers had warned against any light but the moon—she could feel Eli shuffle. A moment later, his fingers brushed hers, then took her hand. Hannah held her breath. What was he going to say? Her chest was tight with anticipation.

Slowly, Eli's thumb stroked the back of her hand. His voice was quiet, so as not to carry in the still night. "I stopped thinking of you as a job a long time ago," he said. "I guess I'm not very good at showing that."

"What do you think of me as?" she whispered, the words almost stuck in her throat. She felt so nervous. Were her hands wet? She hoped not.

"I think of you as a beautiful woman. One who is as beautiful as a rose, with a sweet scent that lures you in, and the thorns for those who get too close or get on your bad side. You're hardworking, caring, a good cook, and someone I sure wish I could spend every minute of my day with."

"Why don't you, then?" Hannah asked boldly. Then, she clamped her mouth shut. What must he think of her now? Forward. Unladylike. Even...wanton?

She could hear the smile in his voice as he answered, "You are a proper woman. I need to court you properly. Before I can do that, I need to help you with this. I took on this job; I want to finish it. There's more, too." He paused for a heartbeat. "I need to protect you, so that I can propose to you."

Hannah put her free hand over her heart. It was sounding loudly in her ears. Could Eli hear it? And if he could, did anyone else? Hannah raised her chin, looking him in the eyes as best as she could in the dim moonlight. Eli was close, so close, the warmth of his body invited her to move closer.

Before she could even blink, Eli's hands were on her face, his lips brushed against hers, and then he pulled back.

Chapter 18

Eli's eyes burned into hers. Hannah shivered, and he drew her closer. "You're a little distracting," he whispered into her hair. "Maybe you should go back inside, so I can keep a look out for danger."

Hannah knew he was right, but she didn't want to leave. Finally, with a small sigh, she nodded, and stepped back slightly. She couldn't just think about herself. She had children to keep safe as well.

Before she could take another step, Eli had closed the distance, kissed her soundly again, and left her breathless as a low whistle sounded, signaling it was time for the men to switch positions.

Gus came around the side, saw her, and shook his head. "You ought to get to sleep," he said.

"I want to be ready if something happens," Hannah argued. "I'm not useless."

"I've a feeling nothing's going to happen," Eli said.

"I'm inclined to agree with you," Gus said.

"But you saw Jethro. He seemed so earnest. He wouldn't have lied," Hannah protested.

"Not saying he did," Gus said. He shook his head. "My worry is that boy got caught or someone followed him here and told his pa. He's not the brightest burning candle."

Hannah hesitated before answering, then reluctantly nodded. "That's true."

"Fact of it is," Gus continued, "if Wallace found out, he'd change his mind and not do anything tonight. So, I think you ought to get some rest."

As much as she wanted to argue against his words, Hannah didn't. They were practical, and honest. Deep in her heart she knew it. She went in, made sure the kettle was filled in case one of the men needed a hot drink, and laid down. She tried to listen for the sounds of anything happening, but after a time, when nothing did, she fell asleep.

When morning came, she fixed breakfast, frying ham and potatoes and onions, and making grits.

The men ate, one eye and ear at all times to the window and door.

"I'm going to saddle up. Ride around and see if I learn anything," Gus said.

"That doesn't seem like a good idea," Hannah worried.

"Bah, Wallace won't hurt me. He's a lot of things, and he gets away with a lot, but hurting an old man? That's something the town wouldn't let go unnoticed. You don't worry about me." Gus set his mug on the table and stood. "I'll go now. Pretend to be checking the fences."

"Want me to come?" Billy asked.

At Gus's nod, Billy jumped up, spooning the last bite in. "Thanks for breakfast, Hannah." He leaned in close to her and whispered, "Don't worry, I'll keep him safe."

Hannah gave him a grateful look. Gavin went to the barn to start chores while Eli entertained Meg for a few moments. The sun was shining, so Hannah decided to take advantage of the fact, and get some of the laundry done.

As she piled it into a basket, Eli appeared, and grabbed it. "I can carry it," she objected.

"So can I. I'm going that way, anyway," Eli told her. He set the basket in the yard near where she washed. "Don't leave this spot. Meg's inside watching over the baby. I told her to keep the door closed so flies wouldn't get in."

Hannah nodded. Then, she closed her eyes. The weight of the last few months was suddenly too much. The tension she'd felt last night at Jethro's warning, and then the fact that nothing had happened at all, was even more difficult to bear.

She opened her eyes to find Eli staring at her, concern on his face. "When will this be over?" she asked softly.

His eyes searched hers. "Hannah," he said, and the way he said her name made her long to fall into his arms for comfort.

He reached a hand out, but then let it fall, and she looked up at him. Would he kiss her again? She wouldn't mind. Was he serious about courting her? Hannah rested her fingers on his arm gently. "Eli," she started.

"Hannah! Lookie here!" Gus's voice shouted.

Confused, Hannah turned, searching for the old man. When she spotted him, she gasped. He and Billy were riding in with a man she not only knew, but had known for a long time, but who also happened to be just who she needed in this moment.

She picked up her skirts and ran toward the riders. Waiting eagerly, she watched as the men dismounted, then threw herself at the third rider. "Uncle Jacob!" she gasped. "Is that you?"

It couldn't be. She hadn't seen Uncle Jacob since the day he'd married her and Jim. What was he doing here?

"My goodness," Jacob said with a grin as he pulled back. "Let me look at you, Hannah. Grown a little, haven't you?"

Hannah couldn't stop the grin that stretched her face. "It's been..." and then she frowned. "Five years?"

Jacob nodded. "Sure has." Then, he looked over at Eli and stuck out his hand. "You must be the man helping Hannah," he said.

Eli shook his hand, and asked, "You are Hannah's uncle?" He gave her a questioning look. "I thought you didn't have any family?"

"I don't," Hannah explained. "Not really. Uncle Jacob isn't really my uncle. He was my neighbor growing up. Jacob Cannon." And then her eyes widened. "And then you became a judge!" Her voice got excited. "Uncle Jacob! Can you help us?"

Chapter 19

Jacob pushed back his plate and shook his head as Hannah hovered a ladle overtop his bowl. "No more, or I'll burst, and I can smell that cobbler you made," he said.

Gavin's head snapped up. "Peach?"

"Peach." Hannah smiled, enjoying the rare grin that spread across his face.

"Now that the meal is over, let's talk business," Jacob said, his face serious. "After some thought, I've decided, I am not the judge for your district, so I can listen and advise you as a family friend without actually risking what's called a conflict of interest in deciding a case."

Hannah nodded, then hesitated. "I hardly know where to begin," she said.

Eli sat, having just given Meg a new animal he'd carved. She wasn't paying attention, too busy having that animal join the others in a line on the floor, which made Hannah glad. She didn't want her daughter to worry.

"I'll tell you," Gus started. "It's that no-good Wallace Carson."

"We can't slander," Hannah scolded him gently. "How does that make us look?"

Gus scowled. "Don't matter; it's the truth."

Hannah set her hand on his arm gently. "It might be, but we are better than that." She set out the cobbler, and as the men helped themselves, she explained quickly the problem with the land ownership, and the fact that Wallace had been threatening her. Gus interjected with his own opinions frequently, while the gunslingers shared their observations on occasion.

Jacob listened with a thoughtful expression, asked a few questions, and after each of them had shared all they knew, shook his head. "Well, Hannah, you have the right to stay. I don't see how any judge could see otherwise, which makes his case against you weak. The real problem seems to be that he's not letting up on the pressure of trying to get you to either marry him or just leave so he can claim the land."

"So what do you suggest I do?" Hannah asked.

"I'm not sure anything that you do will matter," he answered. "The problem is Wallace, and until he's removed, your problem won't be."

"Then how do we get rid of him?" Gus asked. Then, with a quick glance at Hannah, added, "Legal like, of course."

Hannah stood and said, "I am not going to listen to this. You enjoy your cobbler. I'm going to go feed the chickens."

She stepped outside. Breathing in deeply, she let out a sigh and headed toward the back of the house. If Uncle Jacob thought there wasn't anything to be done while Wallace was alive, then that meant it was a likely fact. She couldn't imagine spending the next thirty or forty years—or longer—with Wallace bothering her and out to get her son's land. But that's what was going to happen.

If only there was some way he'd be arrested or punished and be forced to leave her alone. But with the sheriff being one of his family members, and no one willing to speak against him, she knew that wouldn't happen.

She scattered grain for the chickens, then stopped at the garden. The turnips were ready, so she picked a few. The garden looked dry, though. Some of the plant leaves were starting to curl at the edges. She picked up the water bucket. The creek was closer than the well, and it would also give her a chance to see the water level. It had been dry as of late, and it was better to keep as much water in the well as possible, especially with it being clean water, and the only safe one to drink.

Hannah wandered toward the creek. After she watered, she'd take those turnips inside. Some turnip mash would be tasty for lunch tomorrow.

I wonder how long Uncle Jacob can stay. He used to love apple fritters. I think I'll make some of those too.

She kneeled down and started to fill the bucket. A rustling sound came from off to the side, and she tensed. A figure came through a bush, and she rose, preparing to run or scream or both.

When she saw it was Jethro, she relaxed. "Jethro," she said with a smile and a small laugh, "you surprised me." Then, she searched his face. Something wasn't right.

Jethro didn't meet her eyes. His shoulders were slumped, and he didn't say anything. The smile left her face, and her posture tensed again.

"Jethro?" Hannah asked. "What's wrong?"

He looked up at her then, and then back down at his shoes. "I'm sorry, Hannah," he said. "I didn't want to, but Pa—"

Hannah didn't wait for him to finish. She turned, the bucket still in the creek, and started to run. She didn't get far, though. Wallace stepped out of the woods and grabbed her around the waist from behind, pinning her arms.

"Gag her," he ordered his son.

Jethro stepped forward with a dirty rag and wrapped it tightly around Hannah's mouth. She tried to struggle, but it was no good. Wallace was twice her size. She glared at Jethro, but he still refused to meet her expression.

"I'm tired of this, Hannah," Wallace said. "I'm going to get rid of you. I'll keep Meg. She'll be big enough to do the cooking and cleaning soon. I'll raise your boy as my own. It's the Christian thing to do," he chuckled. "Taking in my niece and nephew after their ma dies of sorrow from losing her husband."

Hannah threw herself side to side, hoping to free herself but hardly could move. Wallace shoved her toward the creek, where a pool of water about a foot deep rested, and plunged her into it. Hannah slipped, and struggled to stand. Was Wallace going to attempt to drown her?

"Pa, no," Jethro said. He stepped forward. "You said you wouldn't hurt her."

"And you said you would help me," Wallace snapped.

"Not with this," Jethro said. "Not with...murder."

"It's not murder. It's removing a problem," Wallace snapped. "And you're going to be the next problem removed if you don't help me. Keep a look out."

Hannah struggled, and did the only thing she could do. With her eyes, she begged Jethro for help. For compassion. For anything he could do.

Tears fell from her cheeks as Wallace shoved her back into the creek, pushing her face into the water. He let her up as he turned to his son. "You hear something?"

Hannah thrashed as best as she could. How long would it take to lose consciousness? She fought with all she had, and managed to slip from Wallace's grip. From the corner of her eye, she saw Jethro run toward her house. Was he hiding? Or getting help?

It didn't matter at this point. Wallace was right on top of her now. She got to her feet, but one shoe caught in her apron that was coming loose, and Hannah slipped and fell on her rear, her hands behind her.

Wallace grinned and moved close to her. She was his now, and he knew it. She knew it. There was nowhere to go. Nothing she could do.

Hannah looked around frantically for something to defend herself with.

"I'm going to make you beg to be my wife, just like I said you would," he boasted. "You should have said yes, Hannah. It would have been the smart thing to do. Now, you're going to suffer, and the last thing you'll see is my face."

One hand pulled the gag low. "Never would I have married you." Hannah's voice was firm as she scrambled backward, but then felt the sharp rocks along the edge of the creek press into her back and cut into her hands.

"Aww, helpless little Hannah. Where are your gunslingers now?" Wallace chortled.

"I can look after myself," she hissed. At his smirk, Hannah pressed her lips together, steeled herself, and then kicked out with her foot—aiming for the one place on a man her mama had told her not to touch until they were married.

Wallace hollered and doubled over, rolling in the dirt and sliding into the creek.

That was all she needed. Hannah crawled, then stood, and ran toward the man rushing toward her.

It was foolish of her, she knew it. She couldn't see him. He was too far away, and the setting sun was behind him, making him little more than a shadow. She couldn't hear his shouts over the howling of Wallace, who was trying to chase after her, but she could feel him. Her heart told her he was safety.

Hannah ran as fast as she could, her drenched shoes slipping, her dress catching on low branches that tugged and tore at her. Still, she ran. The man was closer now, yelling something she couldn't make out.

There was a cracking sound, and it took a moment for Hannah to realize it was the sound of a horse whip. She turned around to see Wallace inches behind her, the whip wrapped around his arm and a stunned expression on his face.

Billy stood a short distance away, the whip's handle in his hand and a serious expression, perhaps the first she'd ever seen, on his face. "Don't think so, Carson," he said, and tugged, sending Wallace off balance.

Hannah's feet had kept her moving, and a sudden thud stopped her as arms wrapped around her tightly. She looked up, and cried, "Eli!"

"I told you I'd look after you," he said, and brought her to him for a kiss.

It was too brief. But it completed her. Her heart sang, and she said what she'd been too afraid to tell him. "Eli, I love you."

"I love you too, Hannah," Eli said. He stroked one hand down the side of her cheek. "If you'll have me, I'll never leave you."

"Oh yes," Hannah said, and wrapped her arms around him. They kissed again, then reluctantly, Eli pulled back and looked over to where Billy and Gavin were tying up Wallace.

Gus limped up, holding his back. "Getting too old for this," he grumbled.

Jacob stood, an angry look on his face. Jethro was a short distance away, still looking at his boots.

Hannah watched as her Uncle Jacob went over to Wallace and shook his head. "You made a mistake," he said. "The law binds me into seeing you tried. With my word as evidence, you'll be put away a long time. Might even lose your land."

"Is...is it over?" Hannah asked.

Eli looked deeply into her eyes. "For him it is. For us, it's just beginning."

Chapter 20

Everything seemed to happen in a whirlwind, and Hannah couldn't seem to keep up.

First, Gus and Eli had ridden into town with Uncle Jacob and Jethro, even though it was late. Once he identified himself, the sheriff, relative or not, was cooperative. Especially since Jethro was willing to tell the truth about how his father had been trying to get the land, including the attempted kidnapping, destruction of property, causing "accidents," and almost murdering Hannah.

The next morning, several of the town's women, Mrs. Stover at the helm, had come out in a wagon filled with enough food that Hannah wouldn't have to cook for days. They had cooed over the baby, gifted Meg a new doll, and had insisted on helping Hannah however they could.

She didn't understand it at first, but Mrs. Stover explained that there wasn't a soul in town who didn't feel remorse for not having helped her when she needed it. In fact, several of the old farmhands came and apologized, and offered to help with chores.

Billy thanked them kindly, but sent them on their way. He explained to Hannah that he would help her find new ones, but that she didn't want to hire back people who'd left her at the first sign of trouble. She agreed, but was grateful she hadn't had to say so.

Now that things were calmer, and it was just her, and the children, the gunslingers, Gus, and Uncle Jacob sitting around the table, Hannah felt as though she could finally relax. There was still a lot to figure out, but Jethro had promised he wouldn't be after the land.

"What's going to happen to Wallace?" Hannah asked, then ate a bite of fried potato.

"Jail and or restitution," Jacob answered. "But he won't be bothering you."

She hoped not. Hannah had seen more of Wallace Carson in her lifetime than she ever wanted to see again.

As she was outside a while later, cleaning the dishes, a shadow fell near her, and she tensed, then looked up. Eli stood next to her. "I apologize," Hannah said, and smiled at him. "It's going to take a while before I'm not so jumpy, I suspect."

"That's why I had an idea," Eli said, "if you are willing to hear it."

"What's that?" Hannah asked, drying her hands on her apron. She looked at him expectantly.

"Marry me now," Eli said. "The judge is here. We could do it tomorrow."

Hannah stilled, giving herself a minute to absorb his words. Finally, she asked, "Are you wanting to marry me because I'm feeling jumpy? That would be an extension of your protection?"

Eli tipped his hat back. "I wondered if you'd ask that. No, that's not why." He hesitated, and it struck Hannah that this was the first time she'd ever seen the gunslinger at a loss for words.

She reached out a hand and took his, moving close. "What is it, then?"

Lowering his head, Eli met her eyes, and his expression was fiery. "Because I love you, and I don't want to wait another minute. You, and Meg, and the baby are important to me. I don't want to be without you. I don't want to give you a chance to change your mind if we wait too long. Go for someone else. Someone better."

There was pain in his eyes, and Hannah did the only thing she knew how to do to ease it. She stood on the tips of her toes and brought her face very close to his. "There's no one better," she assured him. "And no one else I'd rather spend the rest of my days with."

Eli kissed her then, and they broke apart only when Gus and Billy started whooping. Hannah laughed, blushed, and turned to the others. "I guess we're getting married," she said.

"I knew it," Gavin said. Then, that rare smile broke across his face.

Meg came running out of the house. "Does that mean you'll stay forever?" she asked Eli as he swung her into his arms.

"That's right," he told her. One arm wrapped around Hannah, and he looked deeply into her eyes. "There's nowhere else I'd rather be."

Epilogue

Six months later

Hannah hummed to herself as she hung out the wash. It was a perfect day. Gus was playing a game of checkers with Meg on a board Eli had made her. Benjamin was napping in a basket in the shade of a tree.

She paused to look off in the distance at the bunkhouse. It was going to be feeling a little lonely soon. True to his word, Billy had found four hard-working farmhands. But that meant that he and Gavin would be leaving soon. The thought made her a little sad.

Of course, the gunslingers couldn't stay forever. They had their own lives to get back to, and had more than extended their stay, citing the fact they would stay until spring to help Eli. But, spring had come, and they'd ridden out with Eli that morning to town. It was only a matter of days before they'd ride out and not return.

Wallace was in a jail no where new Red Ridge, and Jethro had sold the land he owned to Eli. It would stay in the family after all. Her uncle had sent a letter, letting Hannah know she wouldn't need to worry. Neither Wallace, nor anyone related to him, would ever bother her again.

Stopping to check the garden, Hannah nodded in satisfaction at the small seedlings and then picked up Benjamin in his basket and deposited him on the porch by Meg and Gus.

"I'm going to start lunch," she said. "Mind the baby."

Gus grunted, and Meg nodded, but neither took their eyes off the game board. It looked to be a tough match, with each only having a few pieces left.

Hannah was mixing dough when Eli walked in, Billy and Gavin behind him. Eli kissed her forehead and grinned. "Have some news," he said.

"I hope it's good," Hannah said. "I don't like the other kind."

"All depends," Eli said. "We're going to have new neighbors on the east side of the property."

"Really?" Hannah stopped mixing. "Who is it? Do you know?"

"A couple of bachelors. I expect they're looking to settle down," Eli said.

"Mmm. I hope they are not too rough," Hannah said. "Do you think we should invite them for dinner one night?"

"I think so," Billy said, pouring himself some water from a jug. "It's neighborly."

"Make a peach pie or cobbler," Gavin suggested. "I hear that's one of their favorites."

Hannah nodded, and then froze. She stared from one grinning face to the next. "Do you mean…"

"That's right," Billy whooped. "We bought the land today. Fifty acres. Going to build two houses."

"That's wonderful," Hannah gasped, and hugged each of them. "I'm so excited. And Meg will be so happy." It was true. She'd taken to calling them her uncles.

"I've got plans," Billy said. "Got my eye on a girl. Going to see if she'll marry me."

"Got to actually speak to her first," Eli said dryly.

Hannah smacked at his arm. "What about you?" she asked Gavin. "What's making you want to stay?"

Gavin shrugged, and said, "I'm not sure, but I know it's the right decision. Who knows? Maybe I'll find a woman myself. Have what you and Eli have."

Eli rested his hand on his friends' shoulders. "I hope you both get it," he said, then walked to Hannah and put his arms around her. "There's nothing so good as having someone to love."

Hannah melted into his arms. She smiled up at him. As Gus walked in, she said, "I really owe it all to Gus. Without him, I wouldn't have had my gunslinger."

The old man straightened his shoulders, nodded, and said, "Ain't that the truth."

Laughing, Hannah turned back to the mixing bowl. Her heart was filled with happiness, and she could feel it echoing around the room. She didn't know what the future would bring, but she was sure it was going to be something good. How could it not be? She had everyone she loved right here with her.

What's next?

Find out what happens when Billy sets his eyes on the pastor's daughter, but her father is determined to match her with someone who isn't quite what he seems...

Book 2: The Drifter
https://www.amazon.com/dp/B0DQ7HFQ15

***

And if you haven't already, be sure to get your **FREE** book in the Red Ridge Chronicles right here:
https://dl.bookfunnel.com/dt01yp1w38
and join Eli, Billy, and Gavin in the adventure that takes place just before the start of this book.

Note from Author

Thank you for taking the time to read *The Gunslinger*.
Could I ask for one small favor? Reviews like yours on
Amazon mean so much to me and help others to find my
books! Even just a single line means a lot!

Also...

Want a FREE book?

Stop by my website to get your no strings attached **FREE
book**. It's my gift to you, as a thank you for reading this
one.

www.sarahlambbooks.com

Want a Free
Red Ridge Chronicles
Prequel?

Enjoy the gunslingers' adventure that happens just before
Eli answers Hannah's ad.

The Riders

When an old friend calls, legendary gunslingers Eli
Jones, Billy Madison, and Gavin Jefferson answer without
hesitation. They've faced down the toughest outlaws,
always bringing justice with deadly precision and no
remorse. But nothing could prepare them for the fiery
Stella, a woman determined to blaze her own trail—even
at risk to one of their own.

As they race to prevent a catastrophe, the trio soon realizes
that love is a more dangerous adversary than any outlaw.

These quick-draw, sharp-witted gunslingers have always sworn off settling down, but what happens next might just change their minds.

Discover the electrifying prequel to the Red Ridge Chronicles, a historical romance series in ebook, paperback, large print, and audiobook.

Read it in ebook here:

https://dl.bookfunnel.com/dt01yp1w38

Listen to it in audiobook here:

https://dl.bookfunnel.com/bq8tiktnwu

Read or Listen to the Red Ridge Chronicles Books

Amazon: https://www.amazon.com/dp/B0DQ7HFQ15
Audible:
https://www.audible.com/author/Sarah-Lamb/B098H3
SGLK

Book 1

The Gunslinger

Book 2

The Drifter

Book 3

The Lawman

Book 4

The Doctor

Book 5

The Tracker

Book 6

The Newcomer

Book 7

The Old Man

Book 8

The Christmas Rescue

About the Author

Sarah writes captivating characters and clean romance that's anything BUT boring! From heartbreaking moments to heartwarming tales, get swept away in either historical or small town romance that pulls you in until the last page.

Nestled in the Blue Ridge Mountains of Virginia where she's married to her Texan husband, you'll find Sarah creating her next book, homeschooling her two boys, or volunteering in her community.

***

**Want more of Sarah's books? Find them all on
Amazon!
https://www.amazon.com/stores/Sarah-Lamb/auth
or/B098H3SGLK**